BEST
WOMEN'S
EROTICA
2006

BEST
WOMEN'S
EROTICA
2006

Edited by

VIOLET BLUE

Published in the United States by Cleis Press Inc.,
P.O. Box 14697, San Francisco, California 94114.

Printed in the United States.
Cover design: Scott Idleman
Cover photograph: Siege
Text design: Frank Wiedemann
Cleis Press logo art: Juana Alicia
First Edition.
10 9 8 7 6 5 4 3 2 1

ACKNOWLEDGMENTS

First and foremost, thanks, love, and sincere
gratitude go to Frédérique Delacoste and
Felice Newman for the opportunity to become
a part of the fun, sexy, and provocative *Best
Women's Erotica* legacy. It is a deep honor
and a pure pleasure, in every sense. Thank you
for choosing me, encouraging me, inciting me,
and nurturing me.

Hugs and smooches to Chris Fox and Diane
Levinson for all the support a girl could want,
and for being an excellent resource for everything an author needs, plus jokes and smiles
a-plenty.

I would be nothing without friends and
family. Deepest love goes to Survival Research
Laboratories and the Extra Action Marching
Band. Special affection and thanks go to the

head of my family, Mark Pauline, and my dearest friend, Jonno d'Addario.

And to my true love Courtney: thank you for everything you give me, even when we're apart. Everything, always.

CONTENTS

INTRODUCTION:
BUTTERCREAM FROSTING EROTICA

This collection of the best erotica written by women, for women, is meant to be read nice and slow, like a slippery hot afternoon fuck on sweaty sheets, when you don't want to eat... food. The stories are to be carried with you for days after you read them, like sense memories. While compiling this heady collection of hot erotica, I purchased a container of buttercream frosting body butter and wore some behind my ears throughout. Like the delicious sweetness of a warm, fluffy cupcake, a whiff of a particularly memorable story would catch up with me while waiting at a crosswalk for a light to change, or in a quiet moment between kisses. While reading the submissions, I often wished I was in each of these stories; usually I would have to fold up my iBook and flee whatever café I had been working in, too aroused to sit still.

Too much information? I thought it was a sign that I had many good stories to choose from, and San Francisco isn't a bad place for meandering from wi-fi to wi-fi with a laptop, among Victorians and community gardens, with visceral, delicious erotica freshly coursing through my veins. It was a dream come true to become the editor of a series that had been part of my erotic upbringing and an important part of my generation's emerging dialogues on sex. The responsibility loomed, and yet I felt just a little bit punk coming into it as a sexually articulate young woman who had a few unconventional ideas about what she'd like to see in a collection that so boldly proclaims to be the best, the hottest, for women—now. Not that all of the hundreds of stories I received in my call for submissions were sublime; I did reach a point of frustration when I read the twentieth story that started out hot and sweet, then had a breakup, or a death, or a depressed main character. I kept thinking, What the fuck? It's a head-scratcher. Do some people think that "women's erotica" needs to be dark or drama-filled in order to be taken seriously?

I don't think that "literary" erotica, especially women's erotica, needs to be qualified by sadness, anguish, pain, or suffering (unless you mean a tidy spanking). I think that's a holdover from those who believe that because the writing is about sex, it needs to be something more, or less, to be taken seriously as literature.

Together we deliver a message to the publishers, editors, TV writers, and filmmakers who imbue the hot fuck with a moral: you're not relevant anymore. Our erotica is alive. For girls like me, emotional pain and gender stereotyping hinders our hot fucks. We do crazy things and get off like screaming tattooed banshees doing them. We get hard-ons. We suck, we lick, we conquer, we cut and bleed, we cuddle. Our erotica is edgy, yes, but it is joyful. You can wank to it. You want it to happen to you. Its edge comes from authenticity of experience. I get the feeling that a lot of erotica editors try too hard to capture that hunger, that drive that comes from being a real woman on the street, feet on the ground, looking for sex with lips like sugar and a view of the world that's slightly askew, like a familiar puzzle all rearranged to make a new picture. It's a feeling that you experience and can't fake, like a sweet scent you can almost taste, that reminder of your very first warm cupcake.

Take for instance Cate Robertson's "Just Watch Me, Rodin," in which a young woman makes her rent by posing nude for an older male artist who pushes her sexual boundaries, until one day she proves his pushing is no match for her appetite. Slip into the lyricism of Sydney Beier's "Reading to Horst," in which a female American tourist picks up a handsome stranger in a German café and discovers that erotica really is the language of lust. In "The Upper Hand," by Saskia Walker, watch how one clever woman gets the best of the cute young male neighbors who've been spying on her. Rachel Kramer Bussel's "Spike" gives us a comeuppance of a different kind, when a young goth girl shows a pushy "man's man" who wears not just the pants, but the spike-heeled shoes.

When a woman has had enough of the sexual constraints put on her by her lovers and her own ego, she might become her most taboo fantasies (while maintaining a daytime persona that hints at nothing), like the woman in Geneva King's "Utterly Nondescript." Or she might literally push her heightened senses into her headiest sexual fantasies, as does the protagonist in K. L. Gillespie's "Another Assignation with Charles Bonnet." But if she seeks out relief in the manner of Donna George Storey's "Therapy," all bets are off on the outcome of any sexual revelations she might have in store for her hapless therapist.

We go to great lengths to get satisfaction, but if you're like the girl in "Fulfilling Megan," by Bonnie Dee, you'll do whatever's necessary to get off, even if it means making your boyfriend have sex with a stranger for your own gratification. Some couples wind up making strange bedfellows with...fellows, such as the sexually rapacious lesbian couple in Jean Roberta's "The Arrangement." Mired in conflict with a mean (but sexy) boss, any girl is bound to do as the heroine in Elizabeth Coldwell's "Heat," and turn the boiling point of conflict into pure fire. And should the heat become too much, try eating ice cream like the title character in "Consuela" by Alicia Wag, who seduces a young female student and gets her involved in one sticky sexual encounter after another—including one with the male lover she's kept secret.

If you're the kind of woman who pokes around where she shouldn't, especially when it comes to sex, you'll find yourself feeling sympathy spanks for the naughty girl in Eva Hore's "A Spanking Good Time." Or maybe you'll enjoy the predicament in "Busted," by Jordana Winters, where uniform fetishes and public sex collide in one intense, sweaty encounter. Magenta Brown's "Textual Intercourse" goes beyond an adult text operator's sexual clichés and into reality, putting a neat twist on all those "pizza delivery" fantasies. And Teresa Lamai's "In Snow" beautifully blends searing sex and the intricacies of intimacy, culminating in a ballerina's most memorable performance.

Get a taste of several virtual sexual thrills as seen through the eyes of a politically powerful man tired of living through the trysts of others in Lee Skinner's clever "Vicarious." Also tired of wondering if the grass is greener is the woman in "Paid for the Pleasure," by Adrie Santos, who takes a plunge into the world of anonymous ads and allows a man to pay her for his—and her—pleasure. A step further into someone else's sexual world is where L. E. Yates's "Cruising" goes, as a woman who gets off haunting gay male cruising spots gets more than she bargains for when she meets one of her own kind. Turning the tables once more, a dancer takes—and gets—exactly what she wants from the men at a bachelor party in an incendiary group sex scene in "Deal," by Emerald. At the end of it all is Alison Tyler's "Four on the Floor," a triple-X tale of the snarky lovers who hunt for and conquer other couples.

I hope you enjoy the results of me running totally sexually amok putting together the stories in *Best Women's Erotica 2006*. I filled it with erotica that turns my head around and makes me want to fuck, or at least thrust a few fingers in my panties for a little squeeze. Erotica like a stolen fingerful of frosting. Erotica for girls like me.

Violet Blue
August 2005

JUST WATCH ME, RODIN

Cate Robertson

As he has instructed, I knock and enter.

Glancing up from his cluttered, battered old desk, he impatiently motions me in.

"I wish you could be on time for once, Camille," he says wearily. He doesn't want to know why I'm late because he has no interest in me as a person with any kind of life beyond the walls of this sky-lit loft.

I know better now than to protest his calling me Camille. I undress in a corner while he watches me from his desk. Unlike some other men I've worked for, he offers no screen or private space for this part of my job, and undressing in front of him always feels provocative, like stripping. He mentioned once that watching me peel off sparks his muse.

I try not to shiver. It's not that he can't

afford to heat the place. No, I'm sure he keeps it cold deliberately, to make my nipples stick out hard.

He points to the bench, sleek brushed steel and buttoned-down black leather, the single piece of decent furniture in this bright but spartan space. "Do you remember the position? On your back," he says quietly.

How could I forget? Last week, after several sessions of sketching me in an exhausting variety of positions—on, over, around, and even under the bench—he'd finally settled on a conventional fetal pose because, as he said, "It makes your cunt look like a split peach." Besides, any pose must be comfortable enough to hold for forty minutes or more without a break.

I'm just not very comfortable with it right now, hunched here with my forearms clasped lightly around my shins and him stalking around the bench, staring. He goes to the easel, tilts his head; narrows his eyes at me, then at the canvas; then returns to adjust a wrist or thumb here, spread a knee there, untuck the fullness of my left breast from my upper arm.

His fingers on my skin convey energy, like a current or a hum.

He pushes a lock of hair off my forehead and smiles down at me. "Very good, Camille."

By the time he settles at the easel, my cunt is aching.

The canvas is larger than life, four feet high by six feet wide. He paints actively, jabbing and diving and whirling, dancing with it, teasing it, flirting with the paint and the surface. He's all art. Me, I'm just raw material, ore. The diamond-hard point of his gaze drills into me and extracts my essence, claims it for himself, pours it out in an image.

Of me. The way my arse tilts up. He's painting me wide

open. I wonder what possessed me to take this job. This is what I get for dallying in a bar with a cute older guy who turns out to be a big-shot artist. "I need a model," he said. "Want a job, Camille?" Fuck. In for a penny, in for a pound.

The odd thing is that when I close my eyes, I feel the touch of his paint-laden brush on my flesh like a caress. He sees and traces it all, the incurve of my cheek, the contours of my petals, the puckered vortex of my anus. I'm squeezing inside just thinking about it.

Finally, he swirls his brushes into the water: "Time for a break."

In a kitchenette at the back, he makes coffee while I walk around, bend, stretch, jog on the spot, try to dislodge the yawning ache in my cunt. Four times I've been here, naked all afternoon, and he's never offered me a blanket or robe. He brings the mugs and sits beside me on the bench, leaning back, long legs stretched out straight.

I glance at his length, feel his energy close. Clench gently, dewily. Pray that I'm not wetting the leather, or maybe that I am.

He nods at the easel. "Go on. Have a look. It's almost done."

No photo-realist, he's made the splayed, upturned cleft between the creamy thighs fill the canvas with brash, wild color. At first glance, you'd hardly be able to tell that it wasn't the gash of a pitted peach, dripping with juice. Look again, and it's wet, throbbing, joyful, and oh so in your face. My cunt.

For once, I'm speechless. He chuckles. "You like the first in my new series?"

"Series? There's more?"

"Oh, yes. I thought I told you. This is just the beginning.

Each painting in sequence will go deeper into eroticism. Here, you simply display yourself. In the next one—" He pauses. I hardly dare to breathe. "In the next one, you'll touch yourself. And so on."

I try to swallow but my mouth is dry because I'm picturing myself masturbating in front of him. "How many paintings will there be?"

"That depends on you, Camille. How far you can go." His voice is quiet, and he's looking at me now without a trace of a smile.

Yeah, well, you just watch me, Rodin.

After I strip, he says, "No painting today, Camille. Just drawing. Get on the bed. Sit cross-legged. Face the camera."

The bench has been pushed aside for a king-size platform bed made up with a fitted sheet and a pile of pillows in a soft rose pink. I want to question him about the video camera on the tripod, but I keep my mouth shut. He doesn't pay me for small talk.

Bracing his sketchbook on his thigh, he sits on a high stool at the foot of the bed and puts me through several poses, his eyes glued to me, his hand moving as if by remote control, charcoal pencil scratching rough paper.

First, I must throw my head back, cup my breasts and draw out both nipples between thumbs and forefingers. He wants them very erect and red.

"Pinch. Pull harder. Harder," he murmurs. When I wince, he seems pleased.

For the second pose, I lie back on a pile of pillows with my knees bent and spread. On command, I draw my lips apart. I rub and knead. I insert two fingers and then three. I circle and expose my clit rhythmically. He draws nonstop, in patient detail.

I gradually become engorged and very wet. When he stands, I notice the ridge in his jeans and the wet spot just below his belt.

He says, "This last pose may be difficult. If you don't want to do it, I can get someone else."

No damn way, Rodin. "I can do it."

On all fours, I have to present my arse to the camera and press my chest against the bed so that my back is uncomfortably up-arched. Quite the view.

"Spread your thighs," he says quietly. "I'm going to touch you."

With one knee on the bed, he dips his fingers into my cunt and strokes the juices slowly up my crack behind. I swallow to keep myself quiet, hoping against hope that he's going to fuck me now.

But—"Give me your hand." He slips my middle finger into his mouth and sucks it. The one I had up my cunt. Can he taste me? Can he smell me? Then he pulls my arm back at an awkward angle and places the tip of my wetted finger on my anus.

"Press," he says, showing me how. "I want your finger inside up to the last knuckle. Your other fingers should splay against your cheeks like a starfish."

My anal ring tenses, then relaxes at my finger's intrusion. I slide in all the way. I'm breathing so hard that he says, "Move it if you need to, but only slightly." I rock imperceptibly and work my clit with my other hand until my ooze dribbles cool down my inner thighs.

How can he hold back when he sees how much I want it?

But he does. He draws endlessly, while I squirm in misery. Then I hear him get up. Does he move away? I can't tell. With my face in the pillows, I'm not sure where he is, but I sense his presence, and if he's not drawing, what the hell is he doing?

I hold the pose because this is what he pays me for. My thighs are trembling.

In a few minutes, his voice slices through my tension. He sounds breathless, almost winded. "That's enough. Enough for today."

When I know he's gone to make the coffee, I bring myself off hard right there, convulsing with a hand in front and my finger plunging behind. I don't care if he hears my moans.

He brings the mugs. His erection is gone. He clicks the camera off and smiles pleasantly at me.

"You were good today, Camille."

I hope he wanks himself blind when he watches that video.

I almost didn't come back. When I got home and thought about how he made me masturbate in front of him and then jacked off secretly, I was hopping mad. But he sent flowers, no less. With a note on his letterhead. Inside, five twenties. Five times what he pays me per hour. He wrote: *Camille, if I pushed you too far, I apologize for any embarrassment I caused you. Please accept the enclosed as extra payment for the video. I was remiss in not paying you for that up front.—R.*

How could I not come back after that?

I've arrived on time this week. When I hold up my hair behind so he can buckle the velvet choker around my throat, I feel his breath. I swear he caresses the nape of my neck, but maybe I just want it to be a caress. His nails strike sparks off my skin.

He's produced two paintings from the video session, for which I am to pose briefly for final detailing. So I'm here on his bed, reclining into pillows with my clit caught between my right fore- and middle fingers, and my left thumb and forefinger "offering"—that's how he describes it—my right nipple.

"I'm the viewer," he says. "Look at my face. Think, 'I am beautiful. I am me....' No, not like that, Camille. Don't look seductive. This isn't porn. Give me a level gaze. Open to me... That's it! Good girl. Now hold it."

I watch him, at his easel at the foot of the bed, watching me. This isn't porn. This is the body spread open and translated. The luminous essence of flesh, my flesh, in thick, slippery paint. I try to picture him watching me on the video. His face contorted in *le petit mort*. His spunk spewing from the tip of his cock.

During the break, he switches canvasses, cleans and recharges his palette.

Casually: "Do you have a boyfriend?"

"Not right now."

"Fuck-buddy?"

"No. I wish." I roll my eyes: a joke. He doesn't smile.

"Too bad. It would be easier. For the next group of paintings—" he trails off, selecting his brushes. The silence vibrates: I hardly dare breathe. Then his eyes lift and take mine, bore into me. "Would you be averse to posing with a naked man?"

What? Oh, god. I don't know. I stammer. "I don't—think so—who?"

"A friend of mine, another artist."

I gulp. "You want me to fuck him."

He shrugs. "Not necessarily. It's just that it could happen in the poses I want. I'll pay you well."

"I can do that." He shows me the second canvas, tall and narrow, almost finished: me kneeling, from behind. All soft sweep of thighs and intricate cunt-spread curving and shifting into shadow. Lines and planes rise and converge at the still point, just above center. Where my fingers fan open like a sunburst around the middle one, which is buried deep.

Something, some ground inside me, caves in and liquefies. How does he find in an image so outwardly gross a delicacy and fineness so sharp it slices your heart to shreds?

I take up the position on the bed.

He invites me to meet him and Peter for lunch. Café Malu, no less. He introduces me as Camille. Peter is cute and talkative, and wears a wedding ring. For some reason, that reassures me.

When we are back in the studio, it's pen and watercolors, and Peter's good humor is taking a beating. The minute I undressed, he horned up, and he's been stiff ever since. Well, he would be, with the positions Rodin's put us through. But so far the contact has been all external.

Now he wants us doggy-style. For real. He wants a close-up of the entry: how the cock pries the lips open, how the lips wrap around it. The way he talks about it makes me seep. We've all agreed that Peter won't actually fuck me but simply hold his cock at the required depth.

"Need lube?"

"No. Thanks."

Peter kneels close behind, opens my cunt with his fingers, and guides himself gingerly in. Halfway, and Rodin says, "Stop. There. Hold it."

I fight the urge to push myself back, to take him all inside.

Long minutes pass. The pen races, the brush swipes. Page after page. Peter's sweat drops onto my back. His cock is throbbing and I can't help clenching and I know that must drive him mad but I can't stop. We're both trembling, straining to hold back the jungle rhythm in the pulse.

He starts to pant. "Jesus. I'm gonna come."

"Pull out," says Rodin. He passes me a cloth to dry my streaming thighs. "Don't dry your cunt," he says.

Peter fetches three beers from the fridge. "Fuck. I almost blew then, man. I'm gonna get you back for this." He's done this before, I can tell.

After the break, Rodin wants one last position: on a wooden chair, me splayed on Peter's lap with my back to him and his cock securely rooted. He holds my arms, steadies me sweetly, his chest hair soft on my shoulder blades. Rodin kneels right in front of me with his sketchbook. He barks out commands and the pencil flies. No time to think. Just respond.

"Pete, pull her nipples. Perfect.... Pinch her clit.... Grab her hips.... Dig your fingers into her thighs. Higher... Camille, where he enters, touch his shaft. No, a circle with your thumb and forefinger. Good.... Cup his balls... Now play with your clit. That's it. Good girl."

My nipples ache and all I can see is the bulge in his jeans. By the time we finish, my juices drip drip drip off Pete's balls. A little puddle on the seat.

Leaving, I stop at the door and turn. "Can I ask you a question?"

He's cleaning up. He raises an eyebrow. "Sure. Shoot."

"It's probably a stupid question. I just wonder—why do you make me pose live like that? You have a camera. Why can't you just take photos?"

He nods. "It's not a stupid question, Camille. It should be asked more often, in fact. The answer is simple. The camera sees only with one eye. It has no depth perception and it distorts the image very subtly. With two eyes, I have depth perception. I can see what's beneath and behind the surface. I see the whole image, as the camera cannot see it. I bring out the invisible."

As he explains this, something predatory and angular rises inside me, a sharp and bladelike craving. I want to push myself into him.

"And what is invisible?" I ask.

He hesitates. Warily? He wonders where I'm going with this. "Heat. I paint heat."

"Heat? Whose heat?" I press on recklessly, feeling lucky. I want to make him say it. Say, your heat. I paint your heat. Say it, you fucker.

Even across the room, his eyes pin me down. "Mine," he says. "I paint my heat."

For the next several weeks, he paints nonstop, always a couple of canvases going at the same time with several more roughed in. Some days he calls me in to pose, but often he just wants me to be there while he works. Calls me his muse. Right. I feel more like an ornamental house-pet, lounging around on the bed, reading, listening to music, even napping, and always naked. It feels normal. He talks rarely while he paints, but when I make coffee, he takes a break and chats.

One day, he shows me some of the finished work: props the canvases up along the wall.

It's always a shock to see myself painted like this—in fever-ish color, with frenetic brushstrokes, everything vibrating and glowing together. The throb in my cunt radiates from the paint. His work is electric. It looks like fucking feels.

Looking at the paintings, he says, "What do you see?"

I stammer. "Me, but not me. Me, in your eyes." I'm breaking a sweat with the effort.

He says, "Exactly. You in my eyes. How I see you." Now he's looking at me. I can smell him, his sweat, his coffee breath. Did my nostrils flare? No doubt he can smell more than coffee off me.

"Camille, look at me." His face is lined, his eyes magnetic. He's probably my father's age. "I never thought anyone would do what you've done for me. You took on my challenge. And you've performed just as I'd hoped." He pauses. "But—"

Always a *but,* yeah. "I want to push you further."

"How much further?"

"Until you beg me to stop. Until you hit the wall."

I shrug. "What do you have in mind?"

The way his eyes drill into me, I feel my nipples prickle up. "A game. Play a game with me. A game of bondage and domination. Could you do that?" He gives a casual smile, but an undercurrent of tension hums in the air between us.

He wants this. Desperately.

Damn. Damn him. "Sure. I can do that."

When I arrive for the next session, he's laid out some nasty-looking equipment on the bench. I can barely look at it for fear of caving in: handcuffs, a collar, a red ball gag? A blindfold.

A purple butt plug. Something that looks like a small riding crop.

Nipple clamps? Jesus. What have I got myself into?

The video camera is pointing at the bed.

He smiles. "Are you afraid?"

"Yes."

"Good. You should be. It's going to hurt. It has to. But I promise I won't cut you or make any permanent marks on your body. And we'll do this only once. I'll cam it all. And of course I'll make it worth your while."

"Okay." So he's going to pay to tie me up and whip me in front of a camera. Have I now definitely crossed the line from model to whore? Or is this all still for art? I'm not sure anymore. He beeps the camera on.

He buckles the collar around my neck and the cuffs around my wrists. I lift each foot to the bed for him to buckle cuffs around my ankles.

"Kneel on the bed. Facing me, so your hands hang by your ankles."

When he clips the wrist cuffs to the ankle cuffs and I try to move but can't without spreading my knees, I have a revelation: restrained, in this position, my body is automatically designated a sexual object. My raison d'être is crystal clear.

With just a few buckles and clips, he's made me into a fuck toy.

"Now listen. This is important. You won't be able to talk with the gag. We need a safe signal. If you want me to stop, for any reason, stretch out your fingers. Like this. Okay? Good. Now open your mouth."

The ball, though soft, feels huge on my tongue. By the time he buckles it securely in place, my jaw joint is already sore with the strain.

The blindfold is next. Everything goes black and I'm operating by touch and sound. He is quiet for a few seconds. I strain to hear his breathing. Then—"Now I want you to turn over with your face and shoulders on the bed." I obey. Upended. His favorite position for me, but he doesn't say that.

"Are you ready to be spanked?"

I nod, my cheek flattened against the sheet.

Without another word of warning, he hits me with his bare hand, and just after the force of his blow sends fire streaking through my arse and the gag stifles my scream, I wonder if he wonders: how fast will I hit my wall?

I chomp down on the gag. Just watch me, Rodin.

It begins with his hands: slow swipes. Forehand, backhand. With each fiery stroke, I drive my fingernails into my palms and clench the gag in my teeth. Between each pass, he strokes my hips gently, almost lovingly, feathering my skin with his fingertips until I relax with relief, when the next blow knocks me sideways.

I lose count.

"Are you okay, Camille? You're glowing now."

I nod. My face feels flushed and my arse is blazing. His fingers coax sensation back, cool on my cheeks and down over my thighs. Then they creep between my legs and begin to rummage insistently among my petals. He grunts approvingly. I'm oozy and engorged. All that extra blood flow. Everything he's done to me, over so many weeks, all coming to fruition now. I try, but fail, not to rock in response.

He steps away, returns. Something hisses and swoops in the air behind me, makes me startle. The crop. He chuckles. "I want some nice red stripes on this rosiness."

And just like that, he strikes me. *Swoop. Swoop.* Each stroke forces a mangled moan from my lungs. My fists clench and unclench at my ankles as I consider signalling for safety. Again I lose count. But just before I hit the wall, he stops.

I'm struggling to breathe because my nose is so stuffed up. The blindfold feels wet on my cheeks. What is that sound, that muffled sobbing?

Me.

He rolls me onto my back and caresses me, his voice low and soothing, until my breathing steadies and strengthens. "Darling, don't cry. My god, you're beautiful like this. You'll see. I'll show you how lovely you are."

He presses his mouth to my forehead, my cheeks, my breasts. His chest hair brushes me, his cock slides hard and satiny against my thigh. I realize: he's naked. Since when? Since the blindfold? My nipples prick up between his fingers.

"Have you ever had them clamped?"

Before I can shake my head, something bites into the tender, tumescent flesh. One. Two. The pressure is savage and I scream but the sound is strangled. The twin throb of my pinched nipples ignites a relentless pulse down through my clit that makes me buck and grind helplessly. I'm desperate. My body is pleading for release. Begging him.

"Good girl." His voice is tense.

A swipe of thumb between my pussy lips spreads my syrup down and behind. Is that his finger, opening my back hole? Oh sweet fuck. Yes. One. Two. Probing, stretching. I melt down onto him, whimpering. Oh dear god, dear Jesus.

"The butt plug," he murmurs just before he nudges it in. It's solid and it feels huge. My sphincter hugs it so tight I almost explode. But not yet, not until he rolls onto me and and shunts into me rough and deep. When his cock stuffs me full and everything goes numb, I realize I'm dying because I just can't breathe anymore. I hit the wall.

At that instant: the gag is yanked out, the blindfold off. He releases the clamps and fire surges through my nipples and my clit. I'm flung screaming and singing and soaring headfirst through cascades of fireworks into the endless night sky.

I don't know how long I lay there in his arms: until my sobbing and trembling finally petered out and I lay still, shell-shocked. Until evening purpled the studio and hunger won out over exhaustion.

At Malu, my ass throbbed on the chair. I could feel each welt where he'd beaten me.

Where he'd beaten me. Not a sign of the sadist now, in this attractive, middle-aged man of the world sitting across the candle flame from me, stirring his coffee and considering me carefully. Just hours before, this man had cleaved me to my core, ripped apart everything that I thought was me, and put me back together.

"What made it so intense?" I finally asked him. "Was it the blindfold? The gag?"

He lifted an eyebrow and shrugged. "Possibly. Sensory deprivation. When you can't see, your other senses go on high alert. Everything intensifies. When you can't vocalize, everything is bottled up inside. The release was powerful, no?"

Powerful? It was nuclear. I never came so hard.

"Stay the night," he says.

He plays the video and when it is over, he says, "Did you see the beauty in that? How you exploded under me. I want to capture that in paint."

I answer the tense note in his voice with my thigh over his. He fucks me warmly and companionably this time, but sleep is fitful until the gray half-light when he drags me from my dreams to prop me on all fours and slam into me from behind, our bodies clapclapclapping an accelerated applause.

Then a sound sleep, then startling awake at ten-thirty-five with a mid-morning sun baking the bed. Untangling from him and the sheets, fumbling for clothes: "I've got a class at eleven!"

"Easy, darling. I'll give you a lift." Over a cup of his strong coffee, he passes me a thick envelope. Hundreds. A thousand.

"What's this?"

He smiled. "Payment for your services."

"Services? I didn't do anything. All we did yesterday was fuck."

He keeps smiling until it dawns on me.

"If I take this from you, I'm a whore." I put it on the table.

"No. If you take this from me, you're my whore. A whore in the service of art."

He raises a finger to silence my protest. "Camille, listen. Nothing has changed. I pay you to do what I want. What I want changes from day to day. You know that. I've had you masturbate for me. Fake-fuck Peter. In different positions. You've fucked me. Tomorrow I may want you to fuck two men while I watch. But this I can promise you: I will always push you to your limits and I will always want to paint you there."

He offers the envelope again. "You can stop anytime you want. It's all up to you. How far can you go?"

How far? I see the walls stacked three deep with canvases of me, me as sexual energy made flesh, all dark raw wild beauty. Who knew such an erotic creature existed inside me? He draws it out and breathes life into a part of me I never knew existed. Where can he take me? What can he unearth inside me? He's given me a taste.

A taste for more.

I take the envelope with a grin. "Just watch me, Rodin."

READING TO HORST

Sydney Beier

It was finally cooler that day. The last week
held record temperatures for all of Europe and
the German city I lived in hadn't been spared.
I woke at dawn every morning, already panting, my skin glistening with sticky sweat. The
sun rose in the back of my apartment, blazing
through the red window curtains and turning
the entire bedroom pink.

I walked into town for the first time since I
could remember, happy to do some shopping
I'd neglected. The stuffy, crowded shops had
been so intolerable, I chose to do without my
necessities.

My first stop was at a perfume store. I automatically reached for my favorite, Cristalle,
which my husband had been buying me for
years. A pretty woman in the aisle bumped

into me reaching for classic, sophisticated Chanel No. 5. When she had moved on, I grabbed the next one on the shelf. I opened it on my way out of the store and applied some to my wrists, behind my knees, and not caring if anyone was looking, between my cleavage.

I walked up Lothringerstrasse, the bag swinging at my side.

In the middle of the city, just beyond the marketplace crowded with tourists admiring the Dom and Rathaus, was a small park shaded by deciduous trees and a block of apartment buildings. I took a seat on a concrete platform and leaned against a tall, stone monument to Kaiser Karl. Leaves above filtered the sunlight into shadows that danced on my skin and the ground below. The air had thinned in this shaded area and I breathed easier than I had in a long time. I watched a Turkish and an African woman entertaining their children in a nearby sandbox.

I also had a view of the Altenheim on the edge of the park. Nurses in white behind a desk busily checked in visitors and family members. The windows of the home were open and I could hear an old woman inside hollering dementedly, what sounded to me like: *"Fräulein! Fräulein!"*

Her voice dropped from a floor high in the building and mingled with the squeals of the children playing in the park. The little black boy and Turkish girl feverishly arranged sand with a bucket and shovel. They didn't look over at me, but for some reason, I wanted them to. I wanted to see their big eyes and tiny teeth flash at me and to hold the little boy with my hand on his belly like his mother.

The old woman upstairs continued to hoot over and over like an exotic, tropical bird, *"Fräulein!"*

An elderly man emerged from the old folk's home with

two blue parakeets in a white cage. Then another man, about forty-five, strolled across my view of the gentleman with the birds. A little white and brown dog trotted along next to him. They looked pleased on this cool afternoon, taking their time on their walk. The man looked up into the trees with his hands in the pockets of his khaki shorts as the dog familiarized himself with scents along the ground.

Only in the last few years had my attention been directed to older men. Call it a daddy complex, maturity, or aggravation with the inattentiveness and lack of appreciation of the men in my own generation. Older men seem to respect the value of youth, especially that of women. I studied him closely.

I liked his gray hair, slightly grown out and mussed, his slow casual pace, his shape that was big, but solid. I watched his progress through the park and to the street where an automobile from Holland pulled up to the sidewalk and inquired for directions. He threw his hands up in apologetic ignorance.

"I am a tourist," he said in German with an accent I couldn't place.

The car drove off and he continued down the cobblestone sidewalk. Just as another son of the African woman toppled from a bike on which he'd been circling around the park, I rose and brushed the sand off the back of my skirt. The little boy's mother hurried to him in a sweep of bright fabrics. I left her attending to him crying on the ground from a scraped knee. The cling and clang of ceramic dishware at the Café Einstein followed me out of the park.

I'd been reading my new book by Anaïs Nin, recently stocked in the English section at the local bookstore, so I was feeling adventurous and silly. I was also already warm between my legs from her story of a Hungarian baron playing with two girls in the bed of his hotel room. Playing hide and seek with his hard penis under the bedsheets and gazing under their flowing skirts during their roughhousing.

I decided I would follow the man with the dog.

I kept a safe distance down Lindenplatz, then stopped and pretended to dig for something in my bag when the man paused to admire a fountain on the edge of the marketplace. The dog braced himself against the bronze sculpture with his front paws and lapped at the falling water with a flicking, pink tongue.

At the entrance to the marketplace, I again slowed when he stopped to look through the window of a wine shop. I followed him all the way to Dom Keller, one of my favorite student bars. We took seats outside at separate but nearby tables underneath Bitburger umbrellas.

I opened my book flat against the table, hiding the title. I didn't read it, but kept my attention on the man sipping a glass of beer and asking the waiter for water for his dog. I wondered what his story was; why he was alone, why he was in the city, and how I could make contact with him.

I imagined he could see under my table from where he sat, just a few feet away. I had a wild urge to spread my legs and show him how excited I was. I felt that just his eyes resting on me would somehow release the unbearable pressure building up with no outlet.

Germans by nature are a reserved people. Rarely was I aware of men looking at me. If they did, they hid it well. It wasn't like in America where the stares were hungry and uninhibited. There I always knew I had been seen, knew I was alive. It had been so long. I wasn't sure what it was about him that gave me the idea he could change this, but my craving was nearly intolerable. The ice cubes in my water shifted and clinked as they melted in the glass.

Just before I was about to pull my old "my lighter doesn't work" scheme and ask him for his, a group of five university students arrived at the bar and scanned for a free place to sit. It was midday and every table was occupied. The man and I were the only ones alone at tables for four or five people.

Before I could speak up, he did.

The dog stood up when he offered his table to the group and I pretended to be immersed in my book. I feigned surprise when he arrived at my table with the beer in his hand, his dog at his feet, and asked if he could join me.

With an over-enthusiasm characteristic of Americans, I invited him to sit down. He did with a sigh and the dog crawled under the table at my feet to sniff my toes with his cold nose. I giggled and blushed when he licked them. The man looked under the table and scolded the dog teasingly until he complied and plopped down on his belly with his chin between his front paws.

I asked in shaky German what the dog was called.

He said he'd named the dog Thompson.

I asked him what *he* was called.

He said his parents had named him Horst.

My own accent had been a curse during much of my time in Germany. This time it was a blessing. Rather than starting a discussion of all the things he hated about America, he asked where I was from, why I was there, then finally, what I was reading.

I picked up the book and displayed the title for him. He nodded knowingly with a smile and asked if I had read anything by Henry Miller. The yellowed pages were falling out of an old copy of *Tropic of Cancer* sitting on my bookshelf at home. Horst said he preferred Ms. Nin for her softer, more sensual approach. He then informed me that although he understood English, he'd only read their work in German.

Just as I was about ready to ask questions to satisfy my curiosity beyond his name, that of his dog, and his interest in erotic literature, he asked me if I would read to him from the book.

Embarrassed, but compelled, I did. He leaned back in his chair, his hands playing with the base of his beer glass. I looked at him occasionally between passages and he was staring at me intently. My skin prickled under his attention as the words flowed from my lips and stirred excitement in my belly.

The crotch of my panties had been wet since I'd read the story of the baron and I spread my legs a little under the table. The air hit the moisture and cooled the throbbing bloom between them. I imagined that Horst had an erection, but I didn't look to confirm it.

My eyes continued to bounce over the words that my mind and body absorbed. I felt feminine in my skirt, desirable with his attention and hungry with need. The need to be taken, directed, without his asking. I wanted someone—him—to read this instinctually. To pick up the signals I felt I was flashing like high beams.

I figured he thought I was just some nice American girl, reading politely from literature she found poetic, not that it made me wet, my nipples hard, my body aching to be touched, admired, treasured.

I finished the story and took a drink of my water. He thanked me and said it was lovely. He enjoyed being read to and it didn't happen so often now that his wife was gone.

He had a wife?

She died.

I was sorry.

It was a long time ago.

I told him I was married.

I told him the marriage was dead.

I told him it had always been dead.

Funny how easy it is to be completely honest with a total stranger.

He lived alone with Thompson in Heidelberg, but grew up in southern Germany. Now I knew the source of the accent. It had a melody to it, unlike the monotonous drawl of northern Germans. His semester as a university professor was over and he and Thompson were on a little road trip through their country. This was the first city on their tour. They were off to a good start.

I asked him what made him say that. I was tired of the city, thought it ugly and boring. Most of it had been rebuilt cheaply and quickly after the war. The only redeeming features were the ancient cathedral and courthouse in the very center that had been spared by bombs.

He said it was the company of the people he met that he was enjoying most.

I said the people in this city were known to be very friendly.

He said especially beautiful, young expatriates with good taste in perfume.

I blushed and, usually loud and obnoxious, found myself speechless.

The waiter came by and asked if we would like anything else. Horst said no, we'd be paying, and my heart skipped a beat. He gave the man his colorful bills with a generous tip. I remained still and passive, unsure of what was happening and what I should do next.

Horst decided for me. He stood up and offered me his hand. Thompson scurried out from under the table and beat the air with his tail. I accepted the invitation and stood up, grabbing my book and bag with its perfume. He asked if he could buy me dinner and told me his hotel had excellent room service.

I said *yes*.

I was so willing, so eager to please and be pleased; Horst was just the first to detect it and act on it. He was hungry, like me, and the invisible pull of attraction toward one another was overwhelming.

I caught our reflection in shop windows along the sloped pedestrian zone on the way to his hotel and imagined what we would look like if I could step outside of my body and watch from afar. I saw a handsome man with his hand on the lower back of a much younger woman.

She was looking over her shoulder to perhaps see if she recognized anyone in the area. If she did, she didn't care enough to stop. Maybe she didn't think it mattered. No one knew the person she was at that moment anyway.

I could hear his deep voice in her ear, telling her how long it had been. If I'd been able to look through her skin and all the way to her heart, I knew I'd have seen it pumping hard and fast.

Now that I was exactly where I wanted to be, I began to get nervous. I'd never taken a lover before, not since I'd married. I swirled in a flurry of guilt, excitement, anticipation, and worry. Not only had I never had an affair, I had never been with an older man. What if I didn't meet his expectations? What if he didn't meet mine?

I figured once we were through the door to his room, there

would be a flood of activity, clothes dropped to the floor, frantic groping, a serious pounding with a quick ending, and I'd go home, dissatisfaction a familiar acquaintance.

Horst offered me a seat in the armchair in front of the window before calling room service for a bottle of wine and two glasses. It was going to be the other extreme: instead of pouncing on me, he was going to romance me. I thought I might as well enjoy a little bit of attention and fed Thompson a dog biscuit from a bag on the nightstand.

Horst took a seat at the table across from me and again told me he thought I was very beautiful. Without asking, he retrieved my bag and took the book out. He slid it across the table just as a knock at the door announced the arrival of our wine.

While I sat with a glass of wine, a lit cigarette, and the book in my hands, Horst lay on the bed and asked me to read to him again. A few pages into the next story, my anxiety had subsided—until I heard him shuffling. My eyes darted up in time to see him reach for the top buttons of his shirt.

My eyelids fluttered and I sucked in a breath I found impossible to expel.

"Keep reading," he said in English, and I obeyed. Finding my place again, I continued, and my reading accompanied the rustling of his clothing as it was slowly removed and dropped to the floor.

I struggled to keep my place, to pronounce the words, but it became harder and harder as he lay naked on the bed, just feet from me. I kept my legs crossed and squeezed my thighs together.

At last reaching the end of the story, I looked up at him.

He was staring at me with the same intensity as he had back

at our table at Dom Keller. I wondered what he must have been thinking then, if the thoughts had made him hard then like they were now. The pressure in the shaft pulled back the foreskin to expose a plump, spongy tip. It extended up his belly through wispy salt and pepper hair that ran all the way up to his chest.

It was a strange dichotomy: this stranger lying naked so close, and me, still completely dressed and reading to him as if this was a bedtime story. I guess it sort of was.

"One more, please." He grabbed his penis with his hand and began stroking. The wineglass quaked in my hand as I raised it to my lips.

This time, as Anaïs spoke of priests with erections under their robes, Horst slid off the bed and onto the floor. He narrowed the short space between us on all fours. Sitting at my feet, he took one calf, then the other, gently into his hands and removed my shoes. He kissed the arch of my foot and I momentarily lost focus on the print in front of me.

My voice quaked as his hands urged me to rise a little off the chair so he could remove my skirt and panties. I began reading faster, skipping words toward the end. I wanted to finish so I could set the book aside and watch his face in my lap.

His shoulders held my legs apart, his fingers the lips of my sex. Soft, wet slurping sounds emerged from his activity. A blend of my juices and his saliva trickled between the cheeks of my ass and onto the material of the chair. My head dropped back, the book was lost to the floor, my fingers grasped the hair on his head.

He must have sensed my urgency, the feeling that this was too good to last, it has to happen *now*. His hand was warm against my trembling abdomen. It pressed against me, held me steady in the chair as if to say, *There is no rush, no need to hurry, there is plenty more where this came from.*

And I believed him.

I sunk into his mouth, his touch, where there was more of everything: wrinkles, grayness, years, experience, confidence. I was being carried. He just *knew* what to do.

I easily yielded to his pull toward the bed. There he laid me down, spread me out, and slipped inside. Horst was such a big man, full and heavy. I was covered by him, engulfed, my body vibrating with the rumbling moans from his chest. I hadn't come yet, nor had he when he pulled out. I looked down at his penis, glistening in the sunlight coming through the windows. Mouth dropped open, a woman starving, I pulled on his shoulders.

"Ich will—lass mich—" My German was broken, faltering in my dizziness. I wanted, *needed,* to feast on him. *"Bitte."*

He just smiled and slid back down between my legs, escalating my pleasure by denying his own. For the first time ever with a man, I came first.

I found out that day, several times, that an orgasm given without the aid of mechanical devices, my own hand, or the showerhead brought tears to my eyes.

Each climax was different, but I cried through each of them. Horst stayed hard for a long time, long enough to roll me onto my stomach, spread my legs wide and kiss where I'd never been kissed before while working his hand between my mound and the mattress. He held back long enough to pull me on top and guide my hips to grind against him. He finally came when he rolled back on top and rocked his pelvis against mine. I watched his ass thrusting in the mirror until I could no longer keep my eyes open. He kissed my mouth as his body froze against mine.

I woke up next to him at dusk. Thompson was sitting in my chair, looking at me with his head cocked in interest. He lowered his nose to the material on the seat.

When I stood up, I had to hold my hand between my legs to catch all that he had pulled from me and had left behind. It was dribbling out and coating my thighs, making them stick together on my way to the bathroom. I wiped myself with a towel and got dressed in the dark.

Horst was still asleep as I slipped Thompson another biscuit and the book and bottle of Chanel into a side pocket of his travel bag.

I took a route home that passed our table at the bar, now filled with another small group of people laughing and talking.

I walked through the park off the marketplace where I'd first seen Horst strolling with his dog. The women and their children were gone. The windows to the Altenheim were closed against the air that had cooled even further with darkness. Those shadows that had danced at my feet had fanned out and blackened the entire park.

At the pavement in front of my apartment, I looked up to the windows framing the light from inside. I knew my husband was up there.

I took my key out, opened the door with it, and went inside.

THE UPPER HAND

Saskia Walker

Thwack. Lucinda inhaled sharply and counted to ten while she resisted the urge to stand bolt upright. Heat flared through her flesh where the missile had hit her left buttock. She bit her lip and continued to tend her flowerbeds.

"Bloody kids, you'll be sorry," she muttered to herself.

Her neighbor probably had her sister's children over. There'd been laughter and shuffling from over Diana's fence earlier and the missile, whatever the hell it was, had definitely come from that direction. She moved along the flowerbed with her buttock on fire, and then eased upright as gracefully as she could. She wasn't about to let them know they'd hit home, oh no. With kids you couldn't let them get the better of you. Besides, hopping from foot to foot would provide them with no end of amusement.

She collected her gardening basket, pulled her halter bikini top straight, and headed indoors. Once inside, she gave her buttock a quick rub and ran upstairs to the back bedroom, where she had a good view of next door's garden and could spot the little blighters for later public identification. Easing the venetian blinds open a crack, she peeped out.

"I'll be damned…" It wasn't kids at all. Instead it was two rather attractive young men that she spied over the fence. One of them was sprawled in a deck chair looking like a reject from a metal band. Wolf-lean, shades on, with baggy shorts and T-shirt complete with offensive slogan, he had straggly hair to his shoulders and a stack of empty beer cans at his side. The other was on his knees, foraging through the under-growth to spy through a gap in the fence.

"Checking out your target, hmmm," Lucinda murmured, "well, I caught you red handed, you naughty boy."

Because he was bent over in the bushes, she couldn't see too well what he looked like overall, but his rear end was looking pretty good from this angle. Sensing fun, she smiled, her hand going to the exposed part of her buttock, where she'd been hit on a tender spot beneath her high-riding, frayed denim shorts. With a brisk rub of her hand she freed a frisson of sexual pleasure while she took time to observe the view. When the kneeling figure emerged to report to his buddy a moment later, she let her eyes roam over his naked torso. This one was built and built solid. His hair was shaved close to his head, a zigzag pattern delineating the shape of his skull.

"Very interesting indeed," she murmured when she watched him rubbing his hand over the bulge in his jeans, while speaking to his buddy and laughing. They'd obviously been getting off on the view of her rear end while she'd been bent over doing her gardening.

After a good fifteen minutes' observation—during which time she came to the realization that Diana's son must be home from university and he'd obviously brought a friend— she began to formulate her plan to take the upper hand with these two lads, because Lucinda wasn't about to let them get away with it, oh no. She hadn't had the pleasure of meeting Diana's son before, but he was about to find out that his target wasn't shy or easily embarrassed. Star of several explicit art-house movies in the late eighties, and currently director of a South London alternative theater, Lucinda was the type of woman who could envisage the full entertainment potential of a situation like this and had no trouble going after it.

Before she left the upstairs room she hauled her video camera out of the wardrobe and set it up on a tripod, making sure it would catch any activity on the lads' side of the fence, and then she headed back down to the garden, grabbing her sunhat, lotion, and shades on the way out.

The August afternoon heat was simmering; the faint hum of insects in the flowerbeds accompanied her own humming as she strode down the garden. She hauled a sun lounger across the lawn and positioned it just about level with the area of the spy hole. Sitting down, she squirmed into her seat deliberately and began rubbing sun lotion into her arms, alert for signs of attention from beyond the fence. By the time she had covered her arms and shoulders in lotion, she picked up a scuffling sound in the bushes beyond the fence. Smiling to herself, she moved to her legs, kicking off her sandals with panache, being sure to apply the lotion in a seductive and suggestive manner. She thought about having the two lads doing this job instead—one on each thigh. Oh yes, she could just picture it, she could almost feel it. Her hand slid up the length of her inner thigh, massaging as it went.

A suppressed comment emitted from the other side of the fence and a muffled conversation followed. She ignored it, because she didn't want contact yet, she was making this an investment for later. The camera upstairs was whirring and so were the visuals in her mind—they'd be clamoring for a view, she'd be willing to bet on it. Would they both be able to see, she wondered, or would they have to fight over one spy hole, like two young bucks infected with midsummer madness?

She set her bottle down and reached for the ties on her halter neck. When she dropped it she heard another sound. She avoided looking directly at the area of their peephole, but a cursory pass-by under cover of her sunglasses definitely showed movement, and a moment later she caught sight of the crown of the shaved head moving at the top of the fence. They were getting sloppy in their eagerness to see what her breasts looked like. That amused her greatly and knowing she had their full attention, she made a big display of squeezing another puddle of lotion into her palm from a height, dribbling it out slowly. Dropping the bottle, she spread the fluid between her hands and then moved to her breasts. Her nipples were already peaked and she sighed loudly as she spread the creamy liquid over the surface of her breasts, massaging it deep.

They'd be aroused and hard now, cocks pounding, had to be.

Her breasts ached with pleasure and an answering thrum in her groin drew her hand lower, across her abdomen and down, into her shorts.

A stifled groan reached her.

They were watching all right. She wasn't about to stop now.

She decided to watch the video just after sundown, savoring the idea of it while she showered and slipped into a sarong. A large glass of Châteauneuf-du-Pape in one hand and the remote in the other, she settled down on the sofa and flicked the video on.

The camera angle was just right, with just a clip of her in one corner as a reference point. She could see her legs from mid-thigh down and she chuckled to herself as she watched the action begin. The shaved head was clued in to her reappearance by the time she was creaming her thighs and gestured for his buddy to join him. The long-haired one clambered out of his deck chair and over to the fence.

They stood still at first, as if disbelief had them in its grip. Then they were jostling for the best view. As time passed their expressions grew serious, tense. Shaved head turned to say something to his buddy as he pulled his cock free of his fly. They whispered and nodded agreement, then began to hunt around. A moment later it seemed as if they located another peephole and they were both stationed close to the fence, eyes trained on the view, cocks out, occasionally turning to each other to pass comment. They were both masturbating vigorously in the bushes, unabashed by each other's presence.

Fascinating, reflected Lucinda, as she toyed with her nipples through the thin sheath of her sarong.

Shaved head was soon gone on it, rubbing at his cock vigorously, face taut with concentration, eyes narrowed as he squinted through the fence. She took a long draft of her wine and sighed. What an absorbing sight that was and how hot it was making her. She slid off the sofa and onto the floor, closer to the screen, legs akimbo on the rug. She flicked her sarong open, her fingers stroking over her tummy and down, remembering how it had been in the garden, when she'd known she had an audience. She'd always been a bit of an exhibitionist but this was different: they didn't know she knew they'd been watching. Now this was her voyeuristic journey into their arena, their secret wanking, and their laddish camaraderie over the slut next door.

She'd been brewing for another wank and she fingered her slit, imagining it was their eager young male hands on her, as driven as they were over their cocks right now on the screen. Shaved head was stroking himself fast, concentration honed, and then his head went back as a jet stream of come ribboned into the air and splattered on the fence. The toes of her left foot stroked down the side of the screen while she watched wolf-lean one trying to watch through the gap in the fence and wank himself off. What a sight it was when he finally came.

"Oh, boy," she murmured, and thrust harder, her clit bound in pleasure under the pressure of the palm of her hand, two fingers inside, slick and moving frantically. Her sex was on fire, her hips bucking up from the floor. The whirring of the video and the sounds of her pleasure-fuelled sex filled the silent room. And she had the remote; she could fast-forward and rewind just as much as she wanted. Knowing they were so hot for her and being able to watch it over and again was a heady intoxicant and she eked out her pleasure that evening for just as long as she could bear another self-inflicted orgasm.

Diana enjoyed cut flowers. Lucinda preferred to see them growing in the beds, but for the sake of her project she cut an armful and took them round to Diana's the next day. She'd waited until late afternoon, when the lads had taken up residence in the garden and had already downed a few cans of their favored brew.

"They're beautiful, thank you, dear," Diana said as she took the bouquet and ushered Lucinda inside after her while she put them in water.

In the oak and marble kitchen Lucinda gravitated toward the window that overlooked the garden. "It's another glorious day," she commented. Out in the garden the two lads were stretching like waking tomcats, reclaiming their territory, sprawling in the summer warmth. "Oh, is that your son home from uni?"

"Yes, that's Jamie. And the one with the hair," she rolled her eyes, "he calls himself Man, although I don't think that's his real name."

"Man, ay." Lucinda smiled as she watched Jamie cavorting in the sun. He was definitely the showman. And Man was the quieter, long-haired, wolflike one. She was determined to find out what they would be like in closer proximity.

She turned back to her neighbor. "It must be great having two strapping lads around, to help you out with chores and such."

Diana gave a derisive laugh. "Well, I daresay they'd help out in an emergency but they aren't ones to put themselves forward for any task that doesn't instantly appeal to them." She smiled over the flowers, now stashed in a vase. "The garden and the beer seem to have held their attention pretty solidly these past few days. I was out yesterday and when I got home Man had somehow picked up a rash from the bushes and both of them were in danger of getting burnt from overexposure."

Lucinda enjoyed her secret thoughts for a moment. "Are they going to be around for long?"

"Until next week, then they're off to some rock festival in Wales."

"Hmm, in that case would you mind if I borrowed them for an hour or two? I've got one of those self-assembly shelf units that I need a hand with."

"Feel free, I'm sure the offer of a beer or two might sway them."

"I'm sure you're right," Lucinda replied, and smiled. "I'll take your advice and offer plenty of tempting bait."

And she knew just what sort of bait they liked best.

Up close they were just as attractive, if not more so. "Hello, boys," she said, trying to suppress her grin as she noticed Jamie's eyebrows shoot up at the sight of her on this side of the fence. Man shielded his eyes against the sun for a better look. "If it's not too much trouble, I'd like to drag you away from your afternoon sun-worship."

"This is Lucinda, our neighbor," Diana explained. "She needs a hand with some bookshelves; can you two make yourself useful and help her out?"

"I'll make it worth your while," Lucinda interjected.

The two men glanced at each other for support. After a moment they got to their feet.

Once she'd led them round to her place and got them inside, she pointed out the Ikea flat pack in the sitting room and told them she'd get them some beers. Like two hungry hounds that had been thrown a scrap from a plate but sensed the real juicy meat was being kept somewhere nearby, they worked with the chore they'd been given while looking for-lornly in her direction.

The floor was soon covered in packaging, but when she got back their eyes were trained on her. Not surprisingly, she was as provocatively dressed as yesterday, if not more so. She had a great figure for a woman knocking forty years and she knew how to show it off to its best advantage. And she was enjoying every moment of their lascivious eyes on her.

"It's so hard for a single woman to manage a big erection," she said, idly, as she handed them their drinks. Jamie nearly dropped his can; Man swore under his breath and two patches of color appeared on his gaunt cheekbones.

Nice to see we're all on the same wavelength, even if they don't know it yet.

"I really appreciate you two helping me out."

"Any time, Lucinda," Jamie offered, grinning widely, glancing over at his friend and winking conspiratorially.

That was enough of that, she was in control here. She walked over to the sofa and lifted the remote. "Carry on," she said. "I want to see what you make of it." She flicked the video player on.

Dutifully, they turned back to the job they had been assigned to. Lucinda smiled; they were pleasantly malleable and that suited her well. She fast-forwarded through a rather fine BBC production of *The Merchant of Venice* until she felt it was time, and then casually swapped over the videos.

The two of them floundered to a standstill when they caught sight of themselves on the TV screen.

"You were watching us," Jamie murmured.

"I was, but then *you* were watching *me*. Fair exchange is no robbery." Her eyes flicked back and forth from them to the TV. "Quite a sight, isn't it?" she added, raising her glass to them.

"Oh shit," Man declared, flushing when he saw himself wanking on-screen.

"Oh, please, don't be coy. You've got nothing to be ashamed of."

Jamie was a little more in touch with what might be on offer, weighing up what he saw on the screen and what she was showing him: a knowing smile, an enticing glance, a hand nonchalantly linked over the belt of her low-slung shorts, fingers tapping over the zipper.

He set down the assembly instructions he had in his hand. "You knew all along. You went along with it, and filmed it?"

She nodded.

"So why have you brought us round here, really?"

She purred. "Oh, I liked what I saw and I think you owe me a closer look...in the flesh, as it were." She couldn't keep the dirty smile off her face. "You wouldn't object to giving me a repeat performance, up close, would you?"

Jamie grinned. "I'm up for it." He put his hand on the bulge in his jeans. He really did love that cock of his! He turned to his friend. "Manfred?"

Man flicked him a disapproving glance at the use of his full name, but nodded. His lean, hungry looks matched the expression in his eyes.

A bolt of sexual power hit her, pure and powerful. She moved, kneeling up on the sofa. "Right then, I'm sure you won't mind me having a more active role, this time around...?"

They both shook their heads. Man had a wild look in his eyes.

God, this was good! The power rush alone was getting her wet. And they were both sloping closer, hounds with their eyes on the main dish. She had a split second to decide, but she was a very naughty girl at heart and she couldn't resist. She reached into her pocket and pulled out the condom she had stashed there. Flipping it toward the strewn packaging and abandoned shelves she said: "Whoever finds that gets to fuck me; the other has to give me a show."

They stared at her, open mouthed, for a whole five seconds and then reacted, the pair of them scrabbling amongst the cardboard and bubble wrap to find the packet. Lucinda couldn't help chuckling, wishing she had her camera.

Man jumped up triumphantly with the prize in his hands. *Perfect!*

"Oh, bloody hell," Jamie muttered. "That's not fair."

"It is fair; besides, you have no right to complain about anything, since you smacked me on the arse yesterday!"

He pouted.

She pulled her top off, squeezing her breasts in her hands right at him. "Stay where you are. Man, come round here, I want you to fuck me from behind…while Jamie watches." She wriggled her shorts down her thighs, leaning over the back of the sofa.

Jamie's eyes were black with lust. He had his zipper open. He grunted his disapproval when Man took up his position behind her, but started wanking almost immediately. What a sight! A dribble of moisture followed her shorts down her thighs.

"Oh, yes," she moaned. Man had dipped his fingers tentatively into her slit and was stroking his way back and forth from her clit into her wet hole. "Keep going, you're right on target!" He did as requested for a few moments before he cursed under his breath and she heard the sound of the condom being ripped open. She pushed her bottom back, inviting him in, her eyes on the incredible tightness of the muscles on Jamie's arms and torso while he rode his cock with his fist, his hips arched up, his mouth tight as he watched.

Man plowed into her, his cock filling her then rolling in and out, bashing her breasts against the back of the sofa with his urgency. Moments later his fingers groped and hit her clit; she arched again, and his balls hit home. She contracted on him, her body on fire. She groaned and pressed her nipples hard on the sofa, moaning loudly as she hit the jackpot.

"Come closer," she urged Jamie, as she surfaced. He shuffled forward. She stuck her tongue out, and licked the drop of come from the end of his prick. She was starting to come again. He moaned, his eyes frantic. "Come on my tits, baby," she said. He did, a split second later, just as Man exploded inside her.

"You are one hot lady," Man said when he collapsed on the sofa beside her.

"Yeah," Jamie agreed. "I hope you have plenty more *book-shelves* for us to *erect*," he added, with more than a hint of suggestive sarcasm.

"Loads," she confirmed, winking at him approvingly. "But next time I really must film you *getting it up*."

"You drive a hard bargain, but it's a deal," he replied, and Man nodded, laughing.

Not bad for a day's work, Lucinda reflected, and made a note to buy more videotape for her new personal video collection: the upper hand in action.

SPIKE

Rachel Kramer Bussel

The minute I see the shoes, I know I want them. Scratch that—I need them. They are practically talking to me, curving their lips into a gleaming, gooey grin that makes my feet itch to try them on. Their siren song lures me across the store until they are all I see. I pick them up, fondle them, tracing my fingertips along the smooth, supple leather, imagining them on my feet, my feet caressing Jack's cheek, Jack's tongue licking the edges. Their black surface is sleek, shiny, and perfect, crafted to look like a gorgeous piece of art, the kind you might hang on your wall and draw stares for miles, but it's the spiked heels that really do it for me. They are sharp and pointed, like a knife; they could do real damage, both to the wearer and to anyone standing in her way. They are also high; when I try them on, I feel like I've been gifted with those extra inches I've always considered my birthright. I stare down at my feet, not in the mirror, but live, right before my eyes, and know they are right. I march over to the counter, take one off and hold it up to be scanned, then slide it back on, feeling the power wash over me, slowly but quite surely. They hurt when I slip them on, I won't deny it, but it seems a fair trade-off: I'll suffer some pain, he'll suffer more.

Jack was my new lover. We'd only been together once but he'd immediately dazzled me with his ability not only to submit, but to make me want him to do more, to go further into our role-playing until it became less playing and more simply being. Dominance is something I innately warm to, but only under the proper circumstances. I don't walk into a room and instantly want to see every guy there down on his hands and knees. No, it doesn't have mass appeal for me. But when the right guy comes along, watch out. Jack had started the typical macho bullshit with me at some overly hip bar; I wasn't even sure why I'd wandered into the place. He'd teased me about my hair, acted like he'd never seen someone who looked like me: almost goth with my pale skin, jet black hair, tattoos, and piercing gaze. I don't look like the kind of girl you mess with, and when I grabbed his wrist and pulled him into the hallway he started to get the picture. I pushed him up against the wall, my face inches from his. "You don't talk to me like that; nobody does. I think you've just been waiting for a woman to put you in your place. Well, consider me that woman," meaning every single word. He cowered before me, seeming to grow smaller as he saw just how serious I was.

I wormed my fingers under his tight shirtcollar, letting my

knuckles press against his neck, the backs of my fingers hinting at what they could do to his chest. I grabbed one of his hands and thrust it under my latex miniskirt, the kind I manage to pull off as saying "fuck YOU" rather than "fuck me." I rubbed his fingers along the very sheer fabric of my expensive lace panties, then maneuvered them under that veneer, sliding those callused stubs along my wetness. I pulled his fingers back out, then shoved them into his mouth. "You better get used to the way my pussy tastes, because you're going to have my flavor on your tongue for quite a while after tonight." I took a step back. "Say your good-byes and meet me outside in five minutes. I'll be in the red Porsche. If you're not ready, you'll be sorry." And then I did the thing that always throws them off, lures them into thinking that underneath all that gruffness I'm really a nice girl. I winked at him, smiled sweetly and planted a very soft, tender kiss on his big red lips, then pranced back into the bar. I knew that kiss, that sweet, soft mere taste of my lips on his, was enough to make him need to try it again, and try it we did. I spent the entire night teaching Jack a very important lesson about respecting women—specifically, respecting me.

We saw each other several more times before the shoes entered the picture, and each tryst served to cement Jack's position in my life—on his knees, or across my lap; in a word: subservient. It took hardly any time at all to train this tough-talking, macho man into the perfect slave, grateful to do my bidding and getting off on my power over him.

On the date that follows my shopping expedition, armed with my new purchase, we don't waste any time with social niceties. Both of us know exactly why we're here, and that the best way for us to communicate isn't with endless talking, but with his face buried in a pillow or crammed full of my cunt.

That might sound cold, but with Jack, it's amazing how much we each manage to say solely with body language. A sense of calm and strength comes over me the minute I hear him say, "Do whatever you want to me." I feel those words travel from the ends of my hair to my razor-sharp spiked shoes, emitting their own kind of pheromones that quickly swim through my bloodstream, sharpening my resolve. To say I feel maternal toward Jack wouldn't be totally wrong, but the feeling is a combination of so many things. I want to teach him a lesson, but I want it to be my lesson, my way. I want him to walk away from our dates not only with a raw, stinging bottom, his back scraped raw—me having left my mark, as it were—but also knowing that I know what's best for him, because clearly I do.

It takes him mere moments to fully undress and lie down along the length of the couch. His cock is already hard, trying to worm its way between my legs as he wriggles against me. My pussy is wet, but a new kind of wet; not that urging, throbbing hole-needing-to-be-filled-immediately kind of wet, but a wetness that percolates, waiting until the moment is ripe. This kind of wetness could wait, could withstand the slow buildup, could hold out for something better. When I had time to think about it, I considered it a more mature, superior wetness, befitting a woman of my stature.

When he splays himself across my lap, the position feels as if he were meant to fit in the palm of my hand, his little bubble butt poised in the air, just waiting for me. Every babyish quality he possesses surges forth to the surface, his voice going higher, his body seeming to shrink just so, his eyes looking back at me with raw need and hope and urgency, as if I am the only one in the whole wide world who can meet his most visceral desires, and in that second, it's true. I feel like the queen of his world as I run a hand over his face, sticking a finger in his mouth, tracing my nails along his neck, while my other hand tickles the bottom of his foot, then lightly trails up his leg, needing to touch every inch of my newfound domain. I kick out my leg, admiring the way the shoe conforms to my foot, squeezing it just so, the tip darting out in a delicious point. Then I raise my right hand and bring it down across his sweet asscheeks in a way befitting a woman wearing that shoe, befitting a woman with a man splayed across her lap like a baby.

"Unh," he moans, a guttural groan; he's kicking and squirming in delight. I raise my hand again, then land it on one cheek, then bring it up higher, wanting a louder, harder smack. I hold his cheek steady with my other hand, flattening that perfect curve, then bring my hand down again, while he nuzzles his face into the pillow. I keep going, enjoying the sting as it travels up my hand, then, when his sniveling gets to be too much for me, I shove two fingers in his mouth to shut him up. He bites down on them, while I keep increasing my pace, admiring how quickly his ass turns a perfect shade of red. His ass remains what it had been, two perfectly symmetrical rounded cheeks, and yet it also transforms into something else, something softer, subtler, sexier, hard and firm yet open, yielding. I marvel not only at his stamina, but also at his giving, granting me this opportunity to take over, fully and completely, no questions asked, a rarity in our highly regulated world. I stamp my feet on the ground, simply because I can, because right now, I can throw my own temper tantrum, and indeed get what I want, what we both want.

I make him get on his knees, wrists behind him. As I fasten

the pink rope—bought especially for him, because despite
the firm breasts, red lipstick, and spiked heels, I am clearly
the man tonight—around him, he moans again. I love when
he reaches that point of no return, where anything I do, any
decadently dark suggestion I make, is okay. At his finest, I
could bind and gag him, naked, and string him to a telephone
pole, and his cock would be sticking straight up, begging for
more. With his wrists secured, I place him on his hands and
knees in front of me, returning to my throne. That final twist
of the knot has made my pussy twinge, made me start to feel
that more familiar ache that can only be filled in one of a few
ways. I raise my skirt enough for his head to fit underneath it,
and he dives right in, his tongue immediately going to work.
He presses that fast-moving organ deep between my folds,
then brings it back up to mash it against my clit, swirling
in circles and then pressing deep, using his teeth. From his
muffled grunts, I know he's enjoying it, and I look down at
the skirt-covered head between my legs and pat it before leaning back and closing my eyes.

For once, I let myself truly relax, practically feeling my body
unravel, starting with my head. I let my mind go blank, releasing every ounce of tension and worry in my head, then doing
the same from my shoulders on down. Once my precious feet
are loose, hanging in the air as my heels sway, I can suddenly
enjoy his tongue all the more. "Harder," I grunt, because the
truth is, I prefer fingers or dildos or cocks to tongues, but
today, I want his tongue, want him to savor exactly what he's
doing to me. I lift the skirt, pulling it up around my waist until
his mop of hair appears. I beam down at him proudly, knowing I have trained him well; he will only look up at me when
I touch his head and grant him permission.

Under my watchful gaze he works even harder, and best of all, I know for him it's not just work. He enjoys the taste of my twat; truly wants to get me off, and not just because once he does I will very likely allow him to slide his fat cock inside me. He has his own reasons for tasting me, for diving in with boundless enthusiasm, for making his tongue everything I want it to be. He can tell that I'm getting close, and he brings his hand, which has been clasped around my hip, up to my cunt, sliding three fingers in while continuing to torment my clit. I dig my carefully grown, manicured, just-sharp-enough nails into the back of his neck, pressing urgently against the spot I know will make him squirm, then wrap my legs around his back, letting the spikes of my shoes graze his backside, sliding down toward his pert little ass. His fingers slam into me, work overtime, curve and press frantically while his teeth nip at my clit. By unspoken agreement, I buck back against him, thrust upward even as my nails drill his face into my hole, both of us working toward a mutual goal. When I simply can't stand it anymore, I lean my head back, throw my legs wide in the air, and he slides a fourth finger into me, the additional one that makes it a tight squeeze, a little risky, the signal that we've arrived. I scream as my cunt clamps down on him, grit my teeth as my climax races through my body, a comet that burns brightly before its sparks start to fade, leaving us both slightly shaken.

Finally, he looks up at me, the lower half of his face smeared with my juices, his eyes wide and wanting. I slide off one shoe and hold it out to him, and he opens that precious mouth once again, taking the heel between his lips as reverently as one might slide a guy's hard cock between her lipsticked lips. I hold the shoe, don't fuck him back with it, but let him savor the heel that now seems made just for him. I let my bare foot wander to his dick, slide it up and down, fondle his length with the tender, sweaty ball of my foot.

I keep on going, wishing I could tease him all night with the power of my feet alone, no longer needing the threat of the spikes to control him. I'd love to flaunt my power by making him go home with his cock still hard, but I can't do it—not for his sake, but for mine. I want his come, and as I slide both feet now over and around his cock, toying with the head, playing with his balls, my breath comes fast, harsher, in sync with his. He knows this is his reward, but I'm not sure if he knows it's mine as well. I give him my fingers to suckle as he gets closer, and when he's about to come, his sharp teeth come into play, grinding into my fingers, but I don't mind. It's worth a little pain to feel his hot come shoot out over my pedicured toes. He gets another treat when I raise my feet to his lips and let him lick his own come off of them, every last drop. Before he can clean up, he has to massage my feet, then soothe them with lotion before easing them back into the shoes, with which I make my exit. I look down at the heels as they click along the pavement, my clothes only slightly rumpled from our encounter. *Definitely worth every penny*, I think, and give the guy staring admiringly at my shoes a dazzling smile. When I get home, instead of snugly storing them in a box in the closet, I prop them right on top of my dresser, a permanent reminder of just how far I'll dare to go, but only with the right guy—and the right shoes, of course.

UTTERLY NONDESCRIPT

Geneva King

"Last exercise and then we're done for the day." Sue, the leader of today's team-building seminar, beamed around the room at us. A chorus of weak cheers answered her. Most of us were bored to tears, but we'd long learned that if we didn't respond to Sue, she'd try something more sadistic to perk us up.

"I'm going to pass around some papers. There is a different sheet for every person. I want you to write a description of the colleague listed. Likes, dislikes, habits, anything you can think of. Then I'll give the comments out and you can see how you are perceived by your coworkers. Isn't that fun?"

We all filled them out as quickly as possible, then trooped back to our offices. We had finally found a fate worse than work.

I sank into my chair and checked my voice mail. I had one message from my boss.

"Jenny, I need the new shipping forms by the end of the day. By the way, good work on the McNally situation, you handled it well."

The compliment might have held a little more weight if he had gotten my name right. For my first three years on the job, I used to correct him. After that, I just accepted the name of the day. As long as my real name was spelled properly on my paycheck.

I flipped on my computer and got to work. An hour later, I was interrupted by a knock at the door.

"Come in," I called.

Sue poked her head in the door. "I'm not interrupting you am I? Good, I'll just be a minute."

I forced a smile. I had seen about enough of Ms. Chipper to last a while. "Have a seat."

She handed me a pile of papers. "I just came to give you your peer reviews."

I plopped the papers on my desk. "Thank you." I went back to my work.

When she didn't leave, I looked up at her. "I'm sorry, was there something else?"

"Aren't you going to read them? That way we can discuss them."

I didn't want to read the reviews; I knew what they were going to say. Nice girl. Quiet. Keeps to herself.

"Sure, why not?" I picked up the reviews and leafed through them. Sure enough, they said exactly what I had suspected. Nice. Quiet. Wears dark colors. Don't really know her. That roughly translated into plain. Mousy. Nondescript.

Utterly nondescript.

Sue cleared her throat. "One thing I noticed about your reviews was that, while people said nice things, they didn't have much to say. I didn't feel like I know who you are as a person and I don't think your coworkers do either. Now Jayla, isn't it important to you to be a social part of the team?" She gave me one of her smiles.

The phone saved me. "Jayla Stevens, how may I help you?"

"When are you leaving work?" my friend Kim screeched at me. I could tell she was in her car from the sounds of traffic.

"Soon. I have some work to finish. Look, I'm in a meeting. I'll call you when I get home."

"Cool, I have a new spot for us. I want to be out by eleven."

"Okay, bye."

I got up from my desk and walked over to Sue. "Thank you so much for bringing these by. I'll take your advice into consideration. You've been most helpful." I ushered her to the door, guiding her out before she remembered that we didn't actually discuss anything.

I got home with about four hours to get ready for the evening. I should have been tired after a full day of work, but my body was taut with excitement. My work persona was slipping away and my inner vixen was waking up. In another hour, she'd be ready to come out and play.

Off came my black flats, tan pants, and blouse. I unhooked my white cotton bra and stepped out of my high-cut underwear. I threw them in the hamper and hopped in the shower. Tonight, I pulled out my Caress body wash. The scent was sexier than Dove, and it would keep me aroused every time I breathed it in.

Kim had sounded pretty excited on the phone so I dressed carefully. Ordinarily, I'd go for sensual, but after those damn peer reviews, I needed something stronger, something sluttier. I picked an extremely short black skirt and a deep red halter top. If I bent over, my ass would be completely exposed. I decided to forgo panty hose in favor of my crotchless panties. I finished the outfit with a pair of spiky stilettos that showed my freshly painted toes. Red, to match the top.

The last and most important part was my mask. Not an actual mask, so much as eye-catching makeup. It had to be dramatic enough to alter my appearance. When I had the mask on, I was unstoppable. I stopped being nondescript Jayla and became the sexy, vibrant, nasty girl at the party. The girl who would ride a guy until his eyes rolled back in his head. The woman who could take any dick down her throat. She'd fuck a man and lick a pussy, sometimes at the same time.

True to form, we were out the door by 11:00 P.M. on the dot. Kim raised her eyebrows slightly when she saw my outfit. "Rough day?" She knew these trips were therapeutic for me.

I shrugged. "Nothing tonight can't cure. Ready Shelley?"

She grinned at my use of her assumed name. "Let's go, Alexandra."

We took her car, radio blaring Lloyd Banks's album. I rapped along with the CD trying to ignore the sensations welling up inside me. My fingers were tapping on my leg dangerously close to my inner thigh.

"Don't you dare masturbate in my car. These seats are leather. Wait, we're almost there."

We pulled up to a run-down building fifteen minutes later. I smoothed my skirt down before following Kim to the door. What looked like a warehouse turned out to be an underground club. The room was packed with couples gyrating on the floor. There were couches against the walls, and most were filled with people talking or fucking.

As we walked back to the bar, I felt someone grab my leg. I turned around to see a woman smiling at me while a man sucked her pussy. I watched as she closed her eyes in obvious delight, lifting her pelvis to his mouth. One of his hands held the folds of her labia apart, while the other traveled up and down my leg. I knelt beside the woman on the couch and opened her blouse. Pierced nipples peeked out at me and I took one in my mouth. She jumped beneath me, her hands pressing into my head. I flicked my tongue over it then took it between my teeth.

"Yes! Yes!" she groaned.

I paid the same attention to the other nipple and let my fingers caress the one I'd just left. The man found the hole in my panties and slid his finger into my cunt. Her moans were intoxicating and driving me closer to the brink, but I didn't want to come yet. I focused on pleasuring her as he fucked us on the couch.

She smelled delicious. I wanted to taste her, but thought it would be presumptuous to interrupt him. She started to shake and then she came, the juices coursing over his face. I took my mouth from her breast to lick her cum from his face.

"You didn't come." It was a statement, not a question.

I shook my head. "Later."

He stood up and I saw that his dick had sprung free from his boxers. I took his cock in my hands, stroking his shaft while rolling my palm over the head. His eyes closed and he swayed slightly.

"Hold on."

He picked up a condom from the basket on the table. I took it from him and rolled it down his penis, then took him in my mouth. He wasn't that thick, so it was easy to guide him down my throat. It didn't take him long to come. For a second, I regretted that we had used a condom, wishing I could feel his deposit sliding down my throat. But then he pulled out and I got up in search of more adventures.

I looked around for Kim and found her sandwiched between two burly guys on an adjacent love seat. She squealed as one of them peeled her panties off.

I walked on, keeping my eyes peeled for that special something I needed. A guy with a flogger smiled at me, but I shook my head. I needed something else, something nasty, something relentless. And then I saw five dudes chilling in the corner. They looked around excitedly, jabbing each other every few moments. They watched avidly, but didn't make a move to join in. They would do the trick quite nicely.

"Hi." I stepped up to them. Up close, they looked even better. "Wanna fuck?"

They looked completely taken aback. "Uh...yea," one of them managed to choke out. "But who?"

"All of you."

"You want us to run a train on you?" the smallest of the bunch asked.

I nodded. "If you can handle it."

I turned and walked off toward a raised platform I had passed earlier. I grabbed a condom bucket and handed one to each of them. "Suit up. Fuck me good."

I lay down and spread my legs. I purposely left my panties on, to avoid getting the grime of the surface on my ass.

The first guy came up and slid hesitantly into me.

"That's it," I moaned. "Fuck me like the little slut I am."

He moved inside me and I could feel his balls slapping against my butt.

I dug my nails into his shoulders. "Talk to me."

"I'm coming!"

Not exactly what I'd expected. He climbed off and the next guy came on.

"Dirty whore."

"That's it," I yelled. "Fuck me harder."

He growled. "You want this dick? Beg for it, you little slut."

I begged him until he was pounding deep inside me. It hurt, but it was exquisite pain. The kind of pain that drove me closer to the edge. Release was near, but I knew if I rushed it, it would fall flat.

The next two guys were quick, but the last guy stepped up cockily.

"I jacked off before I came here. I can last awhile. Now, turn around ho. I want to fuck you from behind."

I turned over and eagerly backed up onto his waiting cock. He slammed into me, and I clutched the sides of the platform to steady myself. I felt the orgasm coming and I rubbed my clit. Something inside me exploded as I came. I lay limp on the table, but the guy didn't stop thrusting. We fucked until he finished, his climax sending little aftershocks through my body.

They helped me stand and carried me to an empty couch. I reclined gratefully, looking for my friend. Kim was still playing with the guys I'd spotted her with before so I settled down to regain my strength.

My monster calmed, I gave a few more blowjobs and went back to visit the man with the flogger.

We left the club hours later. The sun was starting to rise as we staggered to the car. We turned to an easy listening station to help us wind down.

When I got home, I washed off my makeup and peeled my clothes off, dropping them in the hamper. It would take the remainder of the weekend for Alexandra to fade away. By Monday morning, I'd be Jayla again. Plain. Mousy. Nondescript. Utterly nondescript.

ANOTHER ASSIGNATION WITH CHARLES BONNET

K. L. Gillespie

The smell of rubber tickles my nose and it feels good as I stretch the elastic band out and allow it to snap back on my fingers over and over again. Each time I do it, the rubber band releases a fresh flood of aroma and reminds me of stolen moments from my teens devoted to fumbling and fucking under an old oak tree in the woods behind my house with Jonathan, the boy next door.

The rhythmic snapping hypnotises me like a metronome and the hubbub of my office blurs into white noise as I lose myself and my inhibitions once again under that old oak tree. The sun warms my face and birdsong fills the air. His hands are on my body and his breath is moist on my skin. He pulls out a condom and I can remember its smell and the way it felt between my fingers as if it was yesterday. I helped him peel it on and…

Trng-trng…trng-trng…

The phone starts to ring, ripping through the rose-tinted, sentimental memories of my youth and a sigh begins in the pit of my stomach and escapes from between my lips as I reach out and pick up the receiver, elastic band still in my hand.

It's my mother; she worries about me constantly and phones me often. I struggle to put all thoughts of Jonathan from my mind and hers at rest as she bombards me with a thousand questions. I can understand why she worries, so I tell her I'm fine and pretend I'm going out with friends tonight. She seems satisfied by this and after a few minutes of general chitchat she hangs up.

As soon as I have replaced the receiver I hold the rubber band to my nose and try to recapture Jonathan, but my memories are playing hide and seek with me, teasing me from around corners and mocking me for not being able to picture his face. The harder I try the further away he gets until I am left with nothing but a pile of work to get through before the end of the day.

Five o'clock arrives and I leave the womblike confines of my office and step out into the great big wide world.

The West End's noisy today and even though I've lived here for five years, if I'm not careful I'll get lost so I cement a thousand-yard stare on my face and make a beeline for Charing Cross Station.

The traffic fumes sting my nose and the streets are full of obstacles to overcome. A police car, with its sirens blaring, half circles me as I wait to cross Shaftesbury Avenue and a group of Italians chatter away quickly to my left while to my right an American lazily notices the obvious. A rickshaw whines by and as soon as it has passed I take my life into my own hands and step into the road with a babel of voices ringing in my ears.

The next thing I know a bus whistles past me, taking me by surprise, and as the wind catches my face I gasp, lose my balance and stumble backward.

As I prepare to collide with the pavement I feel arms around me, fingertips pressing into my shoulders, and a distinctive scent enters my nose. Cinnamon. Sweat. Leather. Tobacco. A unique aroma which announces his presence with a bang. I breathe him in deeply, trapping every drop of his essence in my olfactory canal and savouring it slowly before committing it to memory.

This is love at first smell and I am overwhelmed. Suddenly my life becomes a compulsion to make this strange man mine. Unable to resist, I brush my fingers over his hand and a network of nerve endings dance over the surface of my skin, registering the soft warmth of his body and the faint pulse of his life force.

My senses are racing toward overload as I fancy I can taste his strong scent in the air; my mind wanders and I find myself imagining him in my bed, naked and sleeping off a wild night of sex. I would trace his entire body with my fingertips and then I would…

I am dragged back to reality when he removes his hands from my shoulders and I pray now that he has lifted me to my feet he isn't going to just walk away. I still need to hear the sound of his voice to complete the picture and I urge him to speak to me under my breath.

"Are you okay?" he eventually asks, thank god, and his

words vibrate gently in my ears. His voice is deep and warm, like butter at room temperature, and as he speaks to me the rest of the world fades into the background and his utterance fills my head.

I repeat his words over and over in my mind, and I can feel him looking at me, waiting for an answer. My face starts to burn so I break the silence by mumbling something incoherent—but I have no idea what because all I can think of is him, stripped bare between my legs, submitting to my every whim.

Once again my fantasies are cut short when he hands me my white stick and my heart sinks as I sense myself through his eyes for the first time. Out of pity he offers to see me across the road and I hate myself for accepting, but I need more to create him fully in my mind.

I know time is running out so I run through a mental checklist—smell, touch, taste, sound, all accounted for—and then the foreplay is over. He makes his excuses and disappears into the throng but that's London for you, faceless, especially when you're blind.

Nevertheless as I walk away I lift my hand to my lips and I can still smell him on me. He is under my nails and on my skin and I can't wait to get him home.

My train pulls into the station and I search out the nearest door with my stick. I enter an invisible carriage and wait behind a gray curtain for the doors to close and sever my connection with the buzz of the outside world.

As soon as the doors shut I am alone. Everything disappears into a wall of silence, but I'm used to living in an invisible world. I know there are people all around me; someone to my left is eating a burger and the woman in front of me is wearing Poison, but I can't see them and unless I can hear them or touch them they might as well not exist.

I submissively let someone lead me to a seat and count the stops as they pass until the tannoy announces that I have reached my destination. Only another 438 steps to go.

When I arrive home I head straight to the bedroom and begin searching my memory for him but his smell is fading and time is running out so I quickly set about slipping out of my clothes.

As I'm undressing I begin to wish I'd had the courage to run my fingers through his hair and over his face, but I tasted him in my mind after all and as I position myself on the bed I am sure that will be enough to bring him to me tonight.

The soft satin of my bedspread embraces my body as I sink back and recall the sensation of his hands on my shoulders and the taste of him in the air. I lift my hand to my nose again and inhale his odor deep into my lungs, trapping it there until I can hold it no longer. Cinnamon. Sweat. Leather. Tobacco. I run through the memory like a mantra and in the blank darkness I search inside myself for him.

I part my legs and my eager fingertips seek out the triggers that open up the most dormant part of my mind. Quivering with excitement, I conjure him and he appears before me, by the window.

I know he is smiling as he climbs onto the bed behind me and wraps his arms around my naked body. I can feel his sweet breath on the back of my neck like a cinnamon-scented breeze. His pulsating life force warms my skin and as I collapse into him, I place his hand on my breast and shake with delight as he squeezes my nipple between his thumb and index finger. His warm voice murmurs sweet nothings into my ear and I can feel him planting tiny kisses on every notch of my spine.

I can feel his cock hardening in the small of my back and I press myself against it as his hungry hand searches out the cleft between my legs. I arch my back and he slides his fingers into me, holding me tightly by the base of the spine with his thumb. I shiver with anticipation and hold my breath to intensify every flutter and gyration.

As I reach the peak of my pleasure I whisper the secrets of my darkest desires to him and he takes my vulva in his mouth and parts my swollen lips with his tongue. I wind my fingers into his hair and pull him closer until his nose nudges my erect clitoris.

Gently, I rock his head toward me, increasing the rhythm at my body's whim until I am fucking his face with abandon and my senses shift ceaselessly, evoking sight out of sound, smell, and touch. I am about to come but the orgasm is secondary because a miracle is happening.

As I writhe in his arms the gray curtain that shrouds my life begins to disappear and he transports me to a world of light. With a cry of ecstasy I come out of the uncharted void, and for a few seconds colors whose names I don't even know fill my mind and I can snatch them from the darkness. They pulsate in concentric circles like a kaleidoscope and I stare at them in wonder as they shift like curtains in a breeze before my eyes. And they are bright, so bright that I have to narrow my eyes to look at them, but they are the most beautiful things I have ever seen and I drink them in greedily while I can because I know they won't last long, they never do. Then, with a shudder I am plunged back into the darkness.

Sex is my way of seeing and my imagination has a luminous

eye. Passion gives color to my mind and for a few seconds I cease to be imprisoned by my own identity. Every time I do this it ends in a little death and part of me feels sad—because it was such a short affair, like the life span of a mayfly, destined to expire. But tomorrow is a new day and who knows who I will bump into then.

Sleep comes easily. I don't dream but when I wake up my mind is still reeling from the night before. On the way to work my senses are on hyperalert and I realize I am searching for him in every person I pass. I can't concentrate on anything and my appetite, usually so hearty, has jumped ship. Maybe I'm coming down with something. My mother phones and with three questions she has diagnosed my problem. I am in love. It makes no sense in my head but my heart understands, and an hour later I am back on the street where we met, in exactly the same spot, 173 steps from my office and about to cross the road.

I'm still there forty minutes later, sniffing the air, desperate for a hint of cinnamon or a whiff of leather. Waves of musk, citrus, clove, and Brylcreem assault me from every angle but I don't find what I am looking for. He doesn't show and I go home alone.

I'm not hungry so I go straight to bed. For almost an hour I try to conjure him before me again but he is just a shadow that lingers outside my window and refuses to come in. I know he is watching me though, and this quickens my pulse and I slip my hands under the sheets and slowly start to run my fingertips over my naked body. I know the contours of my body better than anything else in the whole world and within seconds I am rushing headlong into seventh heaven. I shut my eyes and will the colors to come, but I orgasm in the dark and it leaves me feeling emptier and lonelier than when I started.

I can't sleep so I put the radio on for company and wait for the morning. The velvet tones of the night time presenter rock me gently but my mind is racing, chasing after the cinnamon man of my dreams. I try to imagine running my hands over his face, tracing the contours of his lips, running my fingers through his hair. It's driving me mad and I know I have to do something about it. I have to try to find him again, starting first thing in the morning.

Sunrise drags its feet and I count the minutes one by one until the alarm goes off.

I rush through work on autopilot, determined to leave early; I was too late the day before and that's why I missed him. It never crosses my mind that he is a tourist, or just passing by—something deep inside tells me that we will meet again, it's just a matter of time.

It's getting late and I've been waiting so long that my feet are numb. I'm beginning to feel faint and my mind has started playing cruel tricks on me. Every now and then I can smell leather or sweat or tobacco but never together, never in that evocative combination that identifies him.

There's a war going on in my head and I'm beginning to listen to my own logic. I know I'm being stupid but rational rules hold no sway over my heart so I continue to stand there, smiling sweetly at every good samaritan who offers to see me over the road; feeling like a fool but refusing to give in.

Suddenly I start reeling with hope and my sixth sense kicks in, forcing me to turn round.

Cinnamon. Sweat. Leather. Tobacco.

He's here. He's nearby. I've been given another chance.

I take a deep breath and turn in his direction. I hear myself saying hello, it doesn't sound like me but I know it's me because the words came out of my mouth. The next few seconds seem to stretch out for hours. I can feel my face burning up and I wish the ground would open up and swallow me.

What have I done? My mind is spinning: Did he hear me? Is he ignoring me? Is he as embarrassed as I am? Is he still here?

Then I hear it, the same warm, buttery voice that melted my heart. He remembers me, he asks how I am, he tells me his name. Charles. I smile and I know he is smiling back. He asks me how I am and if I plan on throwing myself in front of a bus today. I laugh. He laughs. It's all going so well.

He asks where I am heading and I reply; he's going to Charing Cross too and he offers to walk me there. I accept and I know that by the time we arrive I'll be 438 steps away from seeing again.

THERAPY

Donna George Storey

I'm the last person in the world you'd expect to be hurrying through the November dusk dressed like a phone-sex addict's dream girl. It's no lie either. Under my raincoat, I really am wearing a short black skirt, thigh-high stockings, and not a stitch of underwear, not even a camisole under the stretchy blouse I chose especially for the way it reveals my nipples, now painfully taut in the evening chill. Worse yet, gusts of wind are blowing up between my legs, pawing my exposed pussy like a rough, impatient hand.

Fortunately the east side of campus is quiet at this time of day. I haven't run into any of my students, although one man, a stranger, did turn and give me an odd look. "Bit cold tonight, isn't it?" he called out cheerfully. *As if he knew*. Maybe he does. Oblivious as most men are, they seem to have a knack for sniffing out females who aren't wearing panties. Low on the horizon, the full moon's light bleeds into the swirling clouds like the gaze of a probing, silver eye. On an evening like this you can almost believe there is a grander force up there, governing the affairs of the tiny creatures rushing around in the darkness below.

Daniel's office is on the second floor of an old Victorian on Maple Street. The lights are on in his suite, but I see no figures moving inside. As I start up the stairs, a woman walks out, closing the door briskly behind her. She is tall and slim, although at first I can't make out her features in the half-light. Dog or wolf? As we pass, I notice she is in fact quite handsome and her lips are set in a small, secret smile. Of course, it's not proper etiquette to stare at another client at a shrink's office, so I look away. Is it Daniel she's just seen? Daniel who left her with something privately amusing to remember as she glides into the night?

Inside, I take a quick right to the waiting room and snap on the "client has arrived" button next to Daniel's name. I'm too restless to sit down, so I study the fancy carving on the mantelpiece. This room was clearly the visiting parlor in the building's past life as a bourgeois mansion, the place where the young ladies of the house must have received their suitors. I can almost see them in their Sunday finery, lifting teacups to prim lips, pinkies curved. It would certainly bring a blush to their cheeks to see the visitors now, come to confide our darkest secrets to modern-day ministers of the soul.

I hear footsteps. It's Daniel, his forehead creased in a frown. No doubt about it, the man is handsome, his boyish features nudged toward the professorial by a neat golden beard.

"Emma." There's a hint of question in his voice, but he seems glad to see me.

"I hope I'm not too late for a session."

He smiles and shakes his head.

I follow him up the stairway. A faint floral scent lingers— the slim woman's perfume, or perhaps the ghosts of those young ladies descending in their ball gowns.

Daniel is easy on the eye from behind, too. He dresses well: a forest green shirt of soft, fine cloth you want to touch, well-pressed khakis that curve nicely over his firm ass. And then there's that discreet ponytail, a hint of some wilder life. Am I the only one to picture his dark honey hair loose against a pillow, his smooth mask crumpled into a grimace of ecstasy?

Daniel's office is equally restrained: white walls, a bookshelf with titles like *Family Therapy* and *Men and Sex*, a tidy desk in the corner watched over by several framed diplomas. One armchair—his—faces an expensive-looking couch. The scent of leather permeates the room, recalling the tack rooms of my teenage equestrian days, saddles, horse sweat, and some foreign spice, unnamable, but ineffably male.

I lower myself onto the sofa with as much decorum as I can muster in my fuck-me heels.

Daniel remains standing.

"I wanted to discuss something...something I can't talk about anywhere else but here."

Hardly an original opening, but I have to soften him up a bit. *Don't mind me, I'm just like all the rest.* I glance toward his chair. Daniel says he lets the client set the tone for the session. The "expert" doctor role makes him uncomfortable, he claims, although some clients try to corner him into it. True to his philosophy, he follows my cue and sits.

And waits.

Daniel's silence is more than an absence of sound. I should have remembered that. It's an expensive silence, pregnant with significance. Although I have my next move carefully planned, I'm overcome with a desire to blurt out something altogether different: the real reason I'm here tonight.

I glance around the room to get my bearings. The cord of the blinds on the window by his desk has fallen into the trash can, a tiny glimmer of imperfection. I'm tempted to get up and fix it—so tempted my fingers actually twitch—but I resist that particular urge. I look back at Daniel, still waiting, legs crossed. He's wearing his wedding ring today. Sometimes, he says, he takes it off for the first meetings with troubled couples or other clients with conflicted feelings about the institution of matrimony. Did he put it in his drawer for the benefit of the woman who sat in this very spot just minutes ago?

In my nervousness, I've forgotten to take off my coat. I do it now, awkwardly twisting my arms from the sleeves. Unfortunately the room is so warm the thin cloth of my blouse lies chastely over the swelling of my breasts. Even the black miniskirt looks rather tame when I'm sitting down, and I'm not about to spread my legs and show off my other surprise—yet.

His eyebrows lift ever so slightly, but then his expression reverts to impassive calm. No doubt he's probably bored with thirtysomething wives expressing their inner harlot.

So much for my first salvo, but I have more ammunition in reserve and it's best to get started. In here, all you have is fifty minutes, max.

I swallow and soldier on. "I've never talked about this before, but recently I've been troubled by a memory. Of something that happened when I was rather young."

Daniel tilts his head.

"I think it might help if I tell someone. You."

He nods, a careful movement that seems at once encouraging and detached. I wonder, briefly, if they give nodding classes in shrink school.

"May I lie down?" I say.

"If you think you'd be more comfortable."

I stretch out on the couch, my head on the armrest. The skirt finally cooperates and rides up high over my thighs, but strangely enough, the last thing I feel is sexy. The leather is more like a cradle, warming to my skin.

When I rehearsed my story this afternoon before my seminar and a few times before that, my main worry was that I'd giggle and ruin the effect. But here, in front of Daniel, levity has turned to something more like fear. My insides are knotted, my mouth parched and ticklish. I take a deep breath and close my eyes.

"It was the summer after my sophomore year of college. I was nineteen. I'd taken a crappy job at the university library—English majors don't have much to choose from you know—but I took a few weeks off at the end of August to go to my grandparents' farm in Pennsylvania. It beat reshelving books all day, but I was bored out of my mind. Then one afternoon I decided I needed an adventure, so I saddled up their horse, Mitsy, and rode up Peter's Mountain."

Under the veil of my lashes, I check for signs of boredom. Daniel leans forward, the picture of attention.

"I used to ride a lot back then, you know," I continue. "Sometimes guys would make rude remarks about girls on horseback, but the truth is, a saddle doesn't touch the right places. There is something else to it, though. Mitsy was a big bay mare with a rolling gait, and it did give me pleasure to feel such a powerful animal move beneath me, respond to the faintest pressure of my thighs...."

His chair creaks. I don't open my eyes, but my legs suddenly feel hot, *seen*.

"It was very still up on the mountain. Just me, the song of the insects and the muggy heat pressing on my skin. After a while I realized I was riding past a row of huge blackberry bushes, heavy with fruit. There were so many fat berries I just had to reach out and pop one in my mouth. It was sweet. Not like we get in the markets here. You could actually taste the sun in the juices, tiny explosions of crushed berry essence. I ate another, then a few more. I slipped off of Mitsy's back and shoved fistfuls into my mouth while she grazed. I didn't stop until my stomach ached."

A flutter of my eyelids shows me that he is in fact staring at my legs, or rather, at the lacy band that holds the stockings in place at midthigh.

"And then, well, only then did I notice that everything was all too neat and orderly. I wasn't feasting on wild berries, I'd stumbled onto a plantation, someone's property. They raised these things for money. There I stood with my stained fingers and palms. My lips and chin were probably purple, too. A thief caught red-handed."

Daniel chuckles softly. I know he enjoys wordplay.

"I probably should have gotten back on Mitsy and hightailed it out of there, but I was frozen to the spot, waiting for someone to discover me, scold me, force repayment for my theft. But nothing happened. Just birds chirping and the noon sun pounding down and little by little my fear turned to something else. I felt...brazen, for lack of a better word. As if

I were an actor in someone else's X-rated dream and the director was whispering—*go ahead, honey, don't be shy.* Almost in a trance, I pulled the picnic blanket from the saddlebag and spread it out on the ground. Then I took off my halter and shorts, even my underwear, and I lay down, my pale and tender parts exposed to the sun, and I…"

My throat closes around the next word. This isn't going the way I'd planned at all. I meant to unsettle and arouse him, but instead I'm back there again, a naked girl on a blanket, quivering with shame and excitement.

Daniel's patient voice floats into my head as if from far away. "What did you do, Emma?"

I tried to speak, but all that came out was a croaking sound.

"Did you masturbate in the field?"

Did they give classes in that in shrink school, too, saying naughty words out loud with nary a tremor?

"Yes," I squeak. "Funny, I can't seem to say that word here."

"Don't you feel safe?"

"I know I should. But instead I feel nineteen again."

"There is no reason to be ashamed about any of this, Emma."

"But there's more. You see, I didn't do it the usual way, trying to get off as quickly and quietly as I could under the covers. This time I rubbed myself very slowly until I was sopping wet and just about ready to come, then I'd ease off and start again. As if I were daring someone to catch me. Then I saw him…."

"Who?" For Daniel, the timing is uncharacteristically abrupt.

"The workman, the caretaker. In the shadows at the far end of the row. He was watching me."

Daniel sucks his breath, faintly, as if drinking through a straw.

"His hand was moving, about waist level. Up and down. What a normal girl would do, if a normal girl happened to find herself naked on a mountainside jilling off, is cover up and get out of there fast."

"But you didn't."

"No. I spread my legs wider and spit into my palms and circled them over my nipples and made all sorts of sounds in my throat, like an animal. By the end it wasn't even an act. My thighs trembled and my chest was so flushed you'd think someone had slathered berry juice all over my breasts. When I came I groaned so loud, Mitsy walked over and nuzzled me to see if I was okay."

"And the man watching?"

"When I looked over again, he was gone."

"Ah."

"Do you think I'm sick?" I hadn't planned to say that either, but my heart skips two beats as I wait for his answer.

"I don't believe labels are very productive, Emma. 'Sick,' 'exhibitionist,' they're all terms of judgment and shaming. What matters here are your feelings, in particular your desire to have your sexuality be seen and accepted."

I can tell he makes a living at this. But I didn't come here for soothing words. "Isn't it a problem if I act out those feelings? In front of a stranger?"

"It could be, but in this case…"

"You think it was just my fantasy, don't you?" I sit up suddenly.

Daniel's head moves back an inch or two, in what for him must pass as surprise. Is it the strength of my reaction or an unexpected flash of naked pussy?

"I'm not sure that matters so many years later. The scene itself has elements that would be beneficial to explore, whether or not it happened in fact."

"What if I told you I checked afterward and found a puddle of spunk in the grass right where the guy was standing?" In truth I didn't, but I want to keep the engagement on my territory: action, not analysis.

His upper lip curls slightly. Jealousy? A touch of counter-transference?

"I still believe what's most important now are your feelings and why you chose to tell me this today."

I check the clock on his desk, conveniently turned to the couch for the client's benefit. Twenty minutes left and so much more to accomplish.

"Okay, sure, I'll admit most of my sexual fantasies are about being seen and accepted."

"And loved?" Daniel asks softly. "That's what we all want, isn't it?"

I nod. He is good at this. Unable to meet his eyes, I study the Oriental rug that covers the floor between us. The pattern seems backward—the round flowers are like roots, sprouting stems and leaves that beckon with graceful green fingers—*tell me, tell me.* "The truth is I've been thinking about this for a long time. Since the beginning really. I want to do it here. On this couch. I want you to watch."

The room falls into silence.

Except for the taiko drummers, pounding away in my chest and my skull. What started as a joke—repressed hostility as

Daniel likes to say—is now too real. As the moments pass with no answer, it occurs to me that Daniel might actually reject me. Even if he wraps it up in a bandage of professional ethics—*We can't take it that far, Emma, I have a code of conduct in here*—I've offered myself and he's saying no thank you. If only I could disappear, like that workman of fifteen years past, flesh dissolving into phantom. It might happen. Already my thighs are wet against the leather of the couch, melting.

I'm pulled back by a mere whisper.

"All right, Emma. I'll watch you."

As if in a dream, I watch Daniel rise and close the blinds, lock the door against the autumn night. Suddenly it's summer again. The golden light from the lamp on the end table glows like an August sunset.

I pull a towel from my shoulder bag. "Like the blanket I brought for the picnic," I murmur. Plus, of course, I didn't want to mess up his nice couch.

He nods, but with a new air of distraction. The flush on his cheeks and the tent in his khakis suggest he, too, has caught summer fever.

I scoot forward on the couch and part my legs.

Daniel stares. His chest moves rapidly beneath that fine green shirt. "You really aren't wearing underwear. I thought I was imagining it."

I smile and slide my hand over my damp fur, spreading the lips. The click of finger on wet flesh fills the room.

"Do you like looking at me?"

"Yes." His speech is thick, like a drunken man's.

"But you're so used to it, aren't you? Having women show you their private secrets on this couch." Daniel says his real job is asking the hard questions. I'm enjoying this part, turning the tables.

"Not like this," he says.

"But you've thought about it?" I want to hear him say yes. And I don't.

He winces. "Yes, but not the way you think." He keeps his eyes trained on my cunt as if he's explaining himself to her. "It goes a long way back for me, too."

"Why don't you tell me all about it, Doctor?" I begin to rock my hips as I up the tempo on my jiggling finger.

"It's funny, it was also summer vacation when I discovered my dad's girlie magazine stash in the back of his closet. My parents were both at work and I sat there for hours, surrounded by his suits and shirts, the smell of his aftershave, sifting through my treasure."

He pauses.

"Go on," I breathe.

"I couldn't believe it. All of those naked women, splayed out over satin cushions and brass beds, smiling out at me from fur rugs in fire-lit libraries. I remember one girl standing in front of a red velvet curtain, touching her fingertip to the water in a fish bowl that strategically shielded all but one thin crescent of blonde pubic hair. Of course I was turned on. My whole body felt like a huge, throbbing cock. But my head was swimming, too. With questions. What kind of woman would take off her clothes and let men see her? Did she like it? Did that water feel cool on her fingertip? I wanted more of her than flesh. I wanted to go deep inside her mind, her desire."

I moan, low in my throat, even though I've stopped rubbing myself. Daniel's words alone are enough to make my clit throb in sympathy and longing for that teenage boy with a hard-on in his parents' darkened closet. As if I could go back and help him, answer all of his lusts with my own.

For the first time this evening I look straight into his eyes.

"Come inside now," I say.

I expect hesitation. His chair is no more than five feet from the couch, but it marks the boundary between talk and touch, sacred territory here. But he surprises me by practically lunging forward, fumbling at his zipper as he kneels between my legs. He pulls out his cock, sunburn red and weeping a droplet of sea water. Cradling his tool in one hand, he aims carefully, then in another surprise move, thrusts all the way inside me in one stroke.

I grunt and strain forward to grind my pussy up against him, wrapping my legs around his buttocks. His finger dips between us to find my clit, but I shake my head. When I'm this turned on, I don't need it.

"Pull up your blouse so I can see your tits." I like the command in his voice. Apparently he can play Dr. Expert well enough when the mood strikes.

I yank the shirt up to my armpits. My breasts are swollen, mottled with berry juice stain.

"No bra, either, Emma? You do like to show off. And you know how much I like to watch." Daniel smiles and takes one nipple in his mouth and feasts while he rolls the other between his fingers.

I sigh, almost a growl of pleasure. So many sensations, so many dreams fulfilled. Cool, distant Daniel now shaking and sweating, swallowing his moans so his colleagues won't hear. My own body vibrating as he strums the magic strings that join my nipples to my clit. There's nothing left to do but let go, bury my cries in his shoulder, come. Daniel's deep, gliding thrusts tell me he's right there with me. The couch joins in to make a threesome, squeaking faintly in release.

Daniel holds me close until our breathing is steady.

I glance over at the clock. Exactly forty-eight minutes from start to finish. A very productive hour indeed.

As we mop ourselves with the towel and straighten our clothes, I can't help but notice how Daniel's face glows, just the way it did back when we first met. We'd fuck for hours in his grad student dorm, stumbling out of bed at midnight to refuel on pancakes and coffee at the corner diner so we could fuck some more. These days he usually looks tired, with so many clients to see and problems to solve.

I finish buttoning my raincoat and smooth my hair. "One more thing before I go."

He raises an eyebrow expectantly.

I walk to his desk, pick up the blind cord, and arrange it properly outside of the trash can.

"Details, Doctor, details. This has been driving me crazy for the whole hour."

Daniel hooks an arm around me and gives me a quick kiss. "You are a very naughty girl. And always have been."

"Does that mean I need a good spanking?" I wink.

He grins and slides his hand down over my ass.

I pull away, regretfully. "You know if I'm not home by six-thirty sharp, the nanny turns into a witch."

He nods. I can almost see the mask settle back in place. Duty calls us both.

The hall is dark and empty. The air is thinner here, not like Daniel's room, thick with confessions and tears, guilt and pain. Occasionally he talks about his clients—never by name of course—a particularly touching case or a humorous bit of dialogue to amuse me. Still, I can't help but wonder about the things my husband will never tell, the secrets other women share with him, the ways they test him and touch him, if only with words.

Yet such things don't bother me tonight as I float down the stairs, the taste of Daniel's lips lingering in my mouth like fine fruit brandy. I step out on the porch and close the door behind me. Suddenly I realize I'm smiling, but I know exactly why. On this, I'm sure his clients would agree: a little therapy with Daniel always does you good.

FULFILLING MEGAN

Bonnie Dee

"Holy fuck, I've still got a vagina!" I wanted to shout at my boyfriend, Ben as he pumped into my ass crying, "Oh god, it's so tight, so goddamn tight and hot. Fuck. Fuck. Fuuuuuck!"

I had created a monster by suggesting we introduce anal penetration into our sexual diet for a little variety. Ben had so fallen in love with the ass that he was neglecting the pussy. He was gobbling the garnish and had forgotten the main course. The ironic thing about it was that when I first brought up the idea he was totally negative.

"Fuck your poop chute? I don't think so," was his response.

"I believe the preferred term is 'the delectable rosebud of earthly delights,'" I told him. "It's all in your frame of mind. It's supposed to be quite delightful."

"Delightful?" Ben's tone was skeptical.

"Forbidden, hot, naughty, transgressive?" I offered. I couldn't believe I had to sell him on the idea. Weren't men supposed to love the idea of using your back door?

What Ben didn't know was that the ass fuck was only the beginning of my plan to finally fulfill a long-held fantasy. If I couldn't get him to agree to this part, how was he going to feel about taking the next step—bringing a third party into the scene? Slutty or not, my secret desire was to be fucked, front and behind, by two men at the same time. The idea of being the meat in a man sandwich was mind-blowingly sexy to me. My pussy wept just thinking about it and I had reached the point where I couldn't achieve orgasm without my favorite fantasy playing out in my head. Now I wanted to see what it would be like for real.

As it turned out, it didn't take more than one experience to transform Ben into Ass Man, Defender of the Dark Way.

One Friday night I lit the apartment with candles, burned incense, produced a tube of KY jelly and told him, "You're going in."

"Tonight?"

"No time like the present." I started unbuttoning his shirt and pulled it down over his well-muscled biceps, revealing that chiseled chest I loved so much. Ben's body was gorgeous. As I unsnapped his jeans and pushed them down over the sharp blades of his hips, I appreciated the fact that Ben went commando. There was no fuss with underwear; his cock sprang up hard and ready from its thatch of light brown hair. I caressed the long, twitching shaft with one hand and massaged his balls lightly with the other, then I slipped the head into my mouth and slowly sucked the length of it in.

"Oh god, Megan, that's so good!" he murmured, grabbing my head and starting to thrust gently as I bobbed my head up and down.

"And it's only the beginning," I said as I finally pulled off his cock, gave the head a little kiss and turned to position myself on the bed.

I went down on my hands and knees, doggy-style, turning my ass up for his inspection. The idea of being penetrated in the rear was exciting enough to take me a long way toward orgasm, but I had also primed myself earlier by stroking my clit to the edge of coming. My crotch was wet and swollen and hungry.

I felt the coolness of the lubrication and my boyfriend's fingers as he buttered me up in back. Then I felt the bumping of his cock against my anus as if it were knocking and begging admittance. He began to slide it into my body and I felt the pulling, almost burning sensation as my "delectable rosebud" stretched to accommodate his girth.

"Wow. This is...wow," he said, as he continued to press inexorably inside me. "Oh, man."

I smiled and turned my attention to my clit, fingering it lightly, then moving in circles in time to Ben's penetration of my ass. It felt good with him buried inside me; full and kind of odd but good. He began to pull out and I gasped at the sensation.

Ben grabbed my hips and started thrusting in and out of me at his regular pace.

"Easy!" I said. "Slower." I gritted my teeth against the burning. It's hard to explain how it could feel slightly painful but oh so sexy and hot at the same time.

Ben took it easy for about three strokes, then he began

pumping again. "Oh god. Oh fuck. It's so tight, so hot, so gooood!"

Just like that he came. The novelty of the experience and the forbidden nature of it were too much for him. I had to rush to catch up, briskly stroking my clit to a climax.

Ben had collapsed against my back but after a moment he withdrew and flopped down on the bed beside me. "That. Was fucking amazing!" he announced.

Thus Ass Man was born.

Flash forward a month and I was ready to implement the second and trickier part of my fantasy, if Ben was willing. Looking for an opening was difficult but it presented itself when he asked me the simple question, "What do you want for your birthday?"

"You really wanna know?"

He looked at me, curious at my tone. "Yeah. Why? What do you have in mind?"

"Remember when you didn't want to fuck my ass and thought it was kind of gross and freaky?"

Ben made a scoffing noise. "I never said that. I always wanted to do it."

Male selective memory had kicked in but I ignored it. "Well, I have another half to my sexual fantasy. How would you feel about a threesome?"

"Hell yeah!" Ben practically crowed. "That's awesome!"

I instantly recognized my tactical error. "I mean a two guys, one girl threesome."

Ben's face went blank a moment as if he was trying to interpret the words and they weren't computing. "Oh. Well. That's…"

"Not someone we know," I explained. "A stranger. Maybe

even someone we pay. A guy who will do the job and then go away. I really want to try this, Ben. What do you think?"

"I'm not sure I…"

"Please. Picture it, baby. You can watch another guy go down on me or fuck me or watch me suck him off. You can even let him do things to you if you want and nobody we know ever has to know about it. It'll be our naughty little secret. I think it's way hot."

"You really want that?"

"Oh yeah. Like the way you want Angelina Jolie I want it."

"That much?" he grinned.

Ben caved, we found the perfect stranger through the Internet and one night we met the man for a night of fun at the neutral territory of a motel. The seedy atmosphere of the cheap room added to the forbidden nature of the whole affair. I'd never been so turned on by tacky orange and gold drapes and a slippery polyester floral bedspread. The place looked raunchy and perfectly right for our tryst with Mark.

We had found his services online, then checked him out in person at a bar prior to going to the motel to make sure we were getting someone attractive and safe, and we were paying him well for his time. When we got to the motel room Ben poured drinks for everybody to break the ice.

I sipped my whiskey and watched Mark as he slowly undressed, performing a little striptease for us to the sound of the television turned low in the background. As his hot body emerged, I was glad we'd gone with a paid playmate instead of one of the less attractive guys who had responded to our ad willing to participate in our experiment for free.

Ben wrapped his arms around me and leaned in to whisper in my ear. "You sure about this?"

I nodded, unable to take my eyes off Mark.

" 'Cause I'm getting a little wigged," he admitted.

"Look. You play my way and I'll play yours next time. We could hire a girl to do this with us just as easily." I smiled. "Maybe even an Angelina look-alike."

He paused to consider, then stopped objecting. He kissed the side of my neck and reached his hands around to unbutton my blouse and release the clasp on the front of my bra. Plunging his hand inside, he began to fondle my breasts, tweaking my nipples painfully to create two sharp peaks.

"Harder," I whispered, still watching Mark as he shimmied out of his pants and his thick, veined cock was revealed. "Pinch me." I loved it when Ben was rough with my tits. The harder he twisted the more I was aroused and I arched into his hands.

Ben let go of me for a moment while we both shed our clothes and had another sip of whiskey. Then we sat back on the bed and he returned to fondling my breasts. I was between his legs leaning back against his chest and I could feel his hard cock pressing into the cleft of my butt.

Our paid playmate, Mark, was stroking himself to hardness as we watched and suddenly Ben murmured, "Why don't you help him with that? I think it'd be kind of cool to watch you suck another guy's dick."

Relieved that Ben was finally relaxing and ready to experiment, I complied. I beckoned Mark to the edge of the bed and scooted forward. I put my hands on his hips and sucked his half-hard prick into my mouth. We were playing the whole scene sans condoms tonight, having flashed each other STD-free doctor certifications like FBI badges. Plus we were paying Mark a little extra for the privilege of having condom-free fucking. I sucked him in slow and easy so Ben could watch the length of it disappear into my mouth. I heard him breathe in with a little gasp.

I moved my head up and down and wrapped one of my hands around Mark's shaft to stroke in time with my head movements. Spit wet his cock and my hand and lubricated it so I could really get some speed going. One of his hands was clenched in my hair and he was starting to groan with pleasure as I bobbed faster and faster. Then I let go with my hand and swallowed more and more of his length into my mouth, deep-throating him just the way I knew Ben liked.

"Oh god!" Ben gasped as Mark bucked against my face, grabbing handfuls of hair in both fists now. Then he slowed for a moment. "Do you want me to...?" He waited to be given direction as to what we expected from him.

"No man, go ahead and come," Ben said, then added, "On her face. I want to see you come on her face."

Mark resumed thrusting into my mouth for a few more strokes then with a groan he pulled out and aimed his cock at my face, spurting thick wads of white creaminess over my cheeks, mouth, chin, and onto my chest.

"God that's hot!" Ben cried and suddenly I felt more come hitting my back. Ben had jerked off right along with Mark and was on his knees behind me shooting jism.

I was a little annoyed. The whole point of having the two men at once was so that I could achieve double penetration, and now they had both blown their wads within twenty minutes of arriving at the motel. I was dissatisfied and sticky as I watched the guys come down from their orgasmic highs. I went to the bathroom to quickly wash up.

When I returned to the room, the men had turned up the

volume on the TV and were camped out on the bed, watching and talking. I stood with my arms folded until they noticed me.

Guiltily, Ben muted the TV. "I'm sorry, honey," he said. "You, uh, probably didn't get a whole lot out of that, did you?"

"Ya think?" I asked.

"Come here." He patted the bed. I lay down sulkily, but I got over my snit quickly as Mark moved between my thighs and began to lick my clit and Ben snuggled down beside me and began suckling my nipple. While he moved his lips and tongue over one breast, he kneaded the other and twisted the nipple hard the way I liked.

The feeling of being tended to, both breast and cunt, was phenomenal. I moaned my delight while Mark lapped deep between my labia and Ben switched his mouth over to the other breast and pulled on it with strong sucks that bordered on being painful. I looked down through half-slit eyes and watched the two men's heads as they worked my body and felt like Queen Sex of Sexonia.

I felt the first sparklings of my orgasm coiling around inside my clit and building up to a fireworks display, but I didn't want to come like this.

"I want you both inside me," I managed to say in short bursts between the moaning and gasping.

Both men stopped and looked up at me.

"At the same time," I said. This was the one part of my fantasy I hadn't fully explained to Ben. "I want to be completely filled."

Ben sat up, looking surprised. Mark sat up, looking less surprised. I was sure he'd participated in about every possible combination of positions I could think of and probably a hell of a lot I couldn't.

"All right," he said. "Why don't you lie on your side. I think it'll be easiest that way."

I rolled over and without a word Ben fell into place behind me. Seemingly from out of nowhere Mark produced a tube of lubricant and very soon I felt the now familiar coolness of the jelly being spread around and inside my anus. Ben worked one finger, then two, then three in and out of me as I sucked in my breath, totally turned on by the intensity of it. After that I felt his cock, back to rock-hard status, probe where his fingers had just been. He pressed deeper and a little deeper and deeper yet inside me while my body stretched to take him in. Again there was a burning, painful sensation but it only added to the erotic high I was on. My pussy was so wet and aching to be filled I could barely stand it.

Seeing that I was more than ready, Mark lay down in front of me without any more attention to my clit and began pressing his dick into me. I almost came right then. The novelty of a double fuck was such a turn-on. Blood rushed in my ears and I felt my whole body tingling as I was surrounded by male flesh, front and behind. Hands touching me everywhere. Lips on my face, neck, throat. And two swollen, hard cocks inexorably piercing me.

"Gah!" I grunted as they simultaneously began to pull out. I let out a second cry, almost a scream, as they both pushed in again at the same time. It hurt, especially my ass, which wasn't nearly as wide as my cunt. I felt ripped apart, and then was stabbed again as they both thrust once more. Every bit of me was filled. Mark's tongue was even deep inside my mouth and I felt totally possessed. So full of man that there was nothing left of me. I was simply the vessel who had waited forever to be filled so completely.

It was absolutely exhilarating.

"Oh god! More! Harder! Fuck me. Fuck me!!!" I managed to cry. At my cue, both men stopped being slow and gentle.

This time they set up a seesaw rhythm with Ben pulling out as Mark entered and vice versa. Without a word they worked as if choreographed. Fuck front. Fuck back. Fuck front. Fuck back. Both of them were grunting with each thrust and I got it in stereo. The primal sound of their voices elevated me even more. I was about to come. I was peaking. I was coming. Screaming out so loud everyone in the block of motel rooms must have heard me.

My body felt sore and abused by the animalistic fucking but in a good, good, GOOD way that I wanted to go on forever. But the men were just as heated and quickly reached their climaxes too; first Ben, followed seconds after by Mark.

They collapsed against me gasping for air and letting out quiet expletives: "Fuck. Oh my god. That was so good," et cetera. They were covered in sweat. I was covered in their sweat and my own. Come trickled down my thighs onto the bed. We were entangled with each other like one organism with three heads.

I was replete and exhausted and my eyes drifted closed.

"Best birthday ever," I murmured and felt Ben's mouth move in a smile against my neck. He bit the back of my shoulder then subsided onto his pillow again.

A sudden thought occurred to me and my eyes flew open. "But we have Mark for the rest of the night. Maybe there are some other things we should try after we rest awhile."

"Like?" Ben said sleepily.

Mark opened a curious eye.

"Well, guys always want to watch two girls make out and suck each other's tits and pussies. Did you think we don't have the same kinds of fantasies about men?" I asked, rolling onto my back and into Ben.

"Uh, no. Not happening," he declared. "I did this for you but I told you I didn't want any guy-on-guy stuff. Nuh-uh."

"Be-en," I cajoled. "You liked the ass-play, right? And you liked the two-way fuck, correct? Trust me, baby. It's something new for you, but I bet, given enough whiskey, you'll relax and like making out with a guy too."

"Nuh-uh. No way," he repeated.

I rolled back over on my side without an argument, snuggling in between my two hot male bodies and smiling to myself. We had a long night still ahead of us and a lot of whiskey to break down barriers. My newest fantasy had been born and I was determined to see it to fruition.

THE ARRANGEMENT

Jean Roberta

Through the little window in my front door,
I saw the dark wounded eyes of David, my
brother-in-law. Or ex-brother-in-law. I didn't
really know what to call him anymore, but his
eyes could still reach my heart.

He knocked politely, then waited for me to
open the door. I wondered how long he would
stay there if I ignored him, letting him stand
on my doorstep in the dark, in blazing heat,
in rain or in snow, like a faithful dog wanting
in, wanting me. Or wanting my familiar company, I corrected myself, and my resemblance
to the woman we had both loved and lost.

I opened the door with a question on my face.
It was eleven at night, and he had never come
over so late. "I hope you don't mind, Brenna," he begged me. He moved his shoulders

with a kind of feline grace that I thought of as part of his role as an art instructor at the university. He was supposed to have style. He had been dancer slim before, but now he was almost gaunt. "I need to talk to you," he continued.

He had spent a lot of time with me since his wife, my sister Mary the media star, had been killed in a car accident six months before. To the general public, she was a byline in the newspaper, always a source of information. She was never satisfied until the whole truth was out. After her death, I never stopped wishing that she could come back to tell us what it's really like to pass on to the Other Side. The great magician Houdini had promised to send a ghostly message back to the living, if possible. As far as I knew, he hadn't done it either.

I had been soaking in the bathtub while I waited for Allie, my girlfriend, to come home from the hospital. I had thrown my old blue bathrobe around my wet, pink body and felt my tits bouncing as I ran down the stairs to see who was at the door. Even though I was alone in the house, I couldn't stand not knowing.

Now I felt plump and sleazy, like the owner of a rundown boarding house who sweats into a housecoat all day long while surrounded by boarders. I hoped that David wouldn't notice what I was wearing or would make allowances for me because I was almost his sister. As a writer who worked mostly at home, I rarely had to dress for an audience anyway.

I could probably have opened the door stark naked, I thought, and his eyes would never slip below my collarbone. If I must have a straight man in my life, I told myself, I should be grateful that he's such a gentleman.

"You're always so strong," he told me, following me into

the kitchen. I had planned to offer him coffee, but on second thought, wine seemed like a better idea. The bottle of Chablis in the fridge was calling to me.

I held a delicate wineglass in each hand, smiling as I offered him one. I hoped this gesture would compensate for the bathrobe and my damp wheat-colored hair, now drying into its usual messy waves.

"I love your strength, honey," he gushed. Ignoring the gift of wine and taking advantage of my position, he threw his arms around me. His hot, bony chest mashed my nipples flat as his crotch pressed against mine. He felt like pure energy, barely contained by skin and bone. I wondered how he could be so reckless or so naïve; how he could believe that I was made of stone instead of hungry flesh.

I snaked one arm over to the counter and set the wineglass down without spilling a drop. The other glass splashed the back of his shirt as I tried to ease him away from me. "I love you too, David," I babbled, trying to sound sincere but appropriate.

"I want you," he breathed into my hair. "I had to say it. I don't care if—I know you think I'm freaking insane. I know you're a lesbian, Brenna, I'm not ignoring that. You're more than a woman and I'm not a stupid prick."

"David!" I yelped, baptizing him with the rest of the wine. The cold liquid soaking his shirt didn't seem to cool him down. I could hardly believe how contagious his mood was, how it seeped into my skin and all my openings. I felt as if we were both victims of a fateful collision.

"You're not thinking," I explained. "We have to sit down. Take your wet shirt off."

"Okay, okay," he conceded, but tightened his grip. "You're

excited, girl, you know it. You smell good. I could do whatever you want. I'm not a selfish guy. Mary wouldn't blame us."

"You're my brother…," I complained, "…in-law." I pushed forward and he stepped back, still hanging on to me. His hands clutched at my robe, pulling it up. We tangoed toward the front room as my robe inched up the backs of my legs, exposing my thighs. Soon my bare ass would stick out under bunched-up chenille, exposed to his clammy hands. I could smell my own juice.

"I don't want to cause trouble," he sighed against my hot face. His full, smooth lips moved onto mine, and he pressed an urgent kiss on them. His mouth opened.

"David," I said into it, "we have to talk."

"Umm," he answered, pressing his mouth against my open lips and sliding his tongue past my teeth. His long fingers clutched one of my naked buttcheeks, squeezing a message into my flesh. I felt something melt inside me. I moaned, pressing my legs together.

The sash of my bathrobe came undone and he pulled it open. Before I could stop him, he lowered his head to my heaving breasts and pulled a swollen nipple into his mouth. He flicked at it with his tongue, sending waves of electricity into my awakened clit.

I definitely felt like a slutty landlady, and I knew it was too late to redeem myself. He daringly pulled my nipple with his teeth, stopping just short of hurting me, then let go and looked me in the eyes. "I don't want to mess up your life with Alicia, Brenna," he promised. "I'll never marry another woman. I'll probably go back to men."

"You'll WHAT?" I squealed. "Is that your pickup line?"

"Ssh, honey," he soothed me. "Sshh. She knows—knew—

about me. We have an open relationship. We did. I'm just drawn to some guys and some dykes. Wimpy women don't do it for me."

I was standing stark naked in my own front room, my bathrobe in a pool at my feet, while David knelt before me like a knave before his queen. I felt his breath on the bush between my legs before he carefully parted my lower lips, looking for my swelling clit. I wanted him.

The door opened and Allie's vibes rushed into the room like a strong wind. "Where's my—David. Brenna," she remarked, showing the self-control she had developed in her youth as a means of survival. "*Madre de Dios,*" she muttered to herself. No one spoke for a heartbeat. "Is this how you comfort each other?" Allie could resist food more easily than she could resist sarcasm.

David looked at her with an eagerness that I hadn't seen in him for a long time. "Alicia, I don't want to leave you out. I love you women, both of you." He stayed on his knees, looking up.

Allie hesitated, and then I could see the situation pulling her in like a magnet. Tugging her shirttails out of her pants, she strutted slowly to our suitor and tousled his hair. "Are you our hag fag?" she asked him. She swayed her slim hips in his face. "You want to keep up with two dykes, honey, don't expect an easy ride."

I could swear I heard David answer, "Use me."

I didn't want anyone to feel more shocked, degraded, fatally injured or murderously enraged than they might feel already. "Allie, babe," I asked her, "are you sure?"

My sweetie curled her small, determined fist in David's thick hair and shook his head like a terrier playing with a juicy bone. "Oh yes," she told us both, grinning slyly. "We all need it, even if we all have different reasons." She stroked David's face. "She's mine, my man, so I get her first."

Allie grabbed me by the hand and pulled me to the sofa. My breathing speeded up as I realized that David was going to watch her getting me off in her usual ways, and letting me explore all the sensitive parts of her luscious body.

"On your back or doggy-style?" she asked, embarrassing me further. I hadn't expected her to give me a choice.

"This way," I answered, lying on my back. I wanted to see both of them, but I couldn't look at either one for a moment. I held up my breasts, offering them to her and to him.

"Little tease," laughed my girlfriend, pinching one of my hard nipples and rolling it between her fingers. "Help me spread her legs apart," she told David, and he rushed to push my thighs in opposite directions, looking at my glistening cunt lips. Leaning across me, Allie slid an experimental finger in, testing my wetness. Finding me wet and open, she stood up, walked three steps to the corner stand, and pulled a tall white candle from a fancy iron candlestick that was one of our attempts to include art in our lives. Her waxy tool was just thick enough for a first fuck, and she twirled it gently into me, searching for the right angle to push it down into my depths. I moaned, thrusting my hips to show her how much I wanted to be filled. I felt her reclaiming me.

David's strong, bony fingers held my left foot, then he began kneading the sole and running his knuckles across the soft instep. I felt as if I could come from that alone, as tingles chased each other from my foot to my opened cunt. "Oh!" I groaned, feeling as if I could burst out of my skin.

"Brenna," Allie caressed my name as she wielded her candle

in me. "Let go, honey. Give it to us. We want it." I hoped that the hot life exploding in my clit could feed Mary, wherever she was. And my fellow survivors.

Allie gave me a long, deep kiss before helping me up. I noticed that David had shed his clothes, showing the line of dark hair that grew down the middle of his chest to his hard, red cock. His rod was thicker than I expected, and it didn't seem to go with his boyish body. But then, I hadn't seen a cock for so long that anything he showed me would have been a novelty.

Allie swatted him smartly on each buttcheek. She reached around his waist from behind and cradled his balls in both hands as he squirmed and his cock jumped like a puppy. "So you want us both, do you?" she demanded, barely suppressing a guffaw. "What else do you have to confess, bad boy? You might as well tell us. We'll probably find out anyway."

I felt playful, maybe because I seemed to be a universal object of desire. "He likes men, honey," I snitched. I stroked his hard sausage to watch his reaction, and he pulled me close to kiss me.

"Not yet, boy," Allie warned, pulling him back by the hair. I noticed that she liked the feel of it. "So you like cock and pussy both?" She pinched his narrow butt a few times.

He made a noise in his throat, but she didn't let him speak. "Are you confused, David? Or do you feel guilty about your past? I bet you were a tasty morsel for your boyfriends." I remembered that Allie had spent a lot of time with dying patients and their families. She knew that guilt and grief have an obscenely close relationship.

Allie and I were like a sandwich with David as the filling. We pressed against him from the front and the back, swaying in rhythm. She tickled his anus, teasing him with possibilities. "I have a strap-on, dude," she tempted him. "Do you think I'm butch enough for you?"

David groaned. "Alicia," he muttered. "Mistress, please be gentle with me. I haven't had it for years." He moved his butt against her hand while I continued to stimulate him in front.

My sweetie laughed and reached around our toy-boy to hold my hand on his cock. She encouraged me to stroke it, but she held it near the base in a way that prevented him from coming. "You want something, baby?" she taunted.

"Please," he muttered. "Your Ladyship." She ignored his subtle sarcasm, or perhaps it amused her.

"Don't let him come," she instructed me, her assistant, before she walked across the room to rummage in a drawer in our sideboard. Allie returned with a square packet that she ripped open with her teeth to reveal a rolled-up condom in a loud shade of orange. I should have known she would keep medical supplies on hand for emergencies.

Working together, we smoothed the latex raincoat onto David's straining cock. He looked very vulnerable, and I wanted to know if I could comfort him with my mouth. As I knelt to slide my lips over him, I smelled the sharp tang of his sweat, the heat of his private parts. I heard his breathing as I licked him through the tight, slick covering. "Brenna!" he groaned, bucking into my mouth. I held his hips, wanting him to feel my female strength.

Just as she had threatened, Allie strolled out of our bedroom wearing her smaller silicone cock in its light-brown nylon harness that almost matched her skin. By then, David seemed radiant and boneless, willing to surrender in any way we required.

She soon had him on his hands and knees on the carpet. He rested his head comfortably on his arms as we both pressed cooking grease into his tender asshole and on Allie's otherworldly tool. I stroked his back as she slid it steadily into him. I could feel his heart beating under his pumping ribs and glistening skin.

If our versatile Mistress had any doubts about her ability to impersonate a gay male seducer, she hid them well. Somehow I felt as if I were fucking him too, and I couldn't find any jealousy in my heart as she filled a part of him that had been empty for too long.

His grunts and groans seemed more heartfelt than before, and his eruption seemed to come from deeper inside him.

As a reward for offering his ass, Allie let him fuck me. Or maybe this was my reward for waiting patiently for what we had both wanted long before we dared to admit it, even to ourselves.

As he smoothed a new sheath over his amazingly resilient or greedy cock, David sighed, "I've never fathered a child. Ever." This was as close as he could come to protesting our conditions, since he didn't want us to think of him as the kind of gay male vampire who spreads disease among his dearest friends.

The idea of David as a father planted a whole new vision in my mind, my pussy and my guts. I had never had a child either, nor had Allie, but this didn't mean it couldn't happen in the future. We had fantasized about raising a perfect child, or maybe two, a girl and a boy, but our imaginary family had never seemed real to us. The thought drove me to a whole new level of excitement.

"Ohh, Brenna," he gasped in my ear in time to his thrusts, "you love it, don't you?"

I wasn't sure which "it" he was referring to, but I loved what he was doing, so I answered "mm-hm." I'm not much of a talker at such times.

However, I can be quite noisy. As though from a distance, I heard my voice rising to a scream. Allie stroked my hair, bringing me back down from my sweaty frenzy and reminding me that I was still hers.

"I want us to finish off in the bedroom," announced our Mistress of Ceremonies. "I'll bring the rest of the wine." I pulled David by the hand to the stairs that led to our private sanctuary where our beautiful queen-size bed stood in a corner, covered by a handmade quilt, another of our artsy possessions. I realized that our quilt was meant to be a kind of lucky talisman representing Heritage or Roots or Long-Term Commitment, concepts not usually associated with same-sex relationships. I wondered if a straight marriage represented all those things for David.

He began tickling me even before I finished climbing onto the bed, and we rolled around on it like unsupervised kids. I was laughing so hard that tears were rolling down my face when Allie arrived with a tray that carried three glasses and the bottle that now held a pitifully small amount of wine. I wondered whether David could behave better now that he was going to be offered wine for the second time, and this thought set me off on another wave of laughter.

The sight of Allie in the nude sobered me up; the light from our bedside lamps on the planes and curves of her body made her look almost like a statue formed from some precious metal. "You're still full of beans," she told us both, setting the tray on the bureau. "Good. I don't want you falling asleep yet. Who wants the first taste of my love-juice?"

"Me," I volunteered, already tasting her on my tongue. I love the rich shellfish taste of clean pussy, and Allie's has a distinct bouquet that I've become addicted to. David helped me to slide a pillow under her firm butt as she stretched out on the bed, preparing to receive service. She spread her legs, and I buried my head between them, inhaling her scent. While I plunged my tongue into her and tickled her clit with my fingers, David played with her nipples, keeping them hard. She growled in the way she usually does when my attention is getting to her.

I worked steadily on her wet folds while David massaged her shoulders, lightly scratched her arms, and even did some reflexology on her hands. He seemed to have a variety of useful skills that I wanted to learn. I also hoped he would try out all his tricks on me sometime.

We got our Mistress off in style, and I didn't even mind the way she squeezed my head like a walnut between her strong thighs. Of course, she wanted to feel David's tongue as an encore, and she warned him that she expected him to perform like a dyke. The challenge seemed to spur him on.

Allie was so pleased with David that she let him finish her off by trading places with her and letting her ride him to her own grand finale. As far as I could tell, she continued milking his well-worked cock until he came too.

None of us wanted to stop playing with each other, but eventually, the exercise and lack of sleep took its toll on us. We all dozed off in a tangle of arms and legs, sprawled across each other in different positions. The bottle of wine stood untouched where Allie had left it.

I woke up with an urge to pee when daylight flooded the room. Needing relief and wanting answers felt remarkably similar.

I knew I had to shake my two playmates awake so that they could get ready for work, much as they would hate it. Coming back from the bathroom, I watched them sleeping peacefully, and dreaded the thought of disturbing them. They looked artfully arranged, like live models for David's art class. I wondered if he would like to sketch Allie and me, or if we could all take turns taking photos of each other for our private gallery.

Feeling like a spy in the house of love, I poured the rest of the wine into a glass and sipped it slowly, letting it warm its way down my throat. Our three-way arrangement warmed me too, though I knew it would change over time. Nothing living can remain still for long. In this bright morning after, I looked forward to the future for the first time in months.

HEAT

Elizabeth Coldwell

When I think of Ian, I think of heat. The heat
of the sticky days of summer and sweaty sheets.
The heat of the flame that draws in the moth.
The heat of passion, and shame. I think of that
sultry August night, and the things he did to
me, and I still hate him—and I still want him.

I took the job at the Red Mill because I
needed the money. We've all done it—poxy
jobs for poxy pay that kill your self-esteem but
keep the nasty letters from the bank manager
at bay. Trouble is, most of us do it when we
leave school, or to help us get through a degree
course, not when we're knocking thirty, like I
was. You don't need to hear the sob story; all
you need to know is my nice, safe marriage
and my nice, safe job in retail management bit
the dust at roughly the same time, and I found

myself living in a rented bedsit with damp in the kitchen and a DIY-fetishist landlord who spoke a dozen words of English and whose idea of fun was drilling holes in the walls at eleven at night. Bar work at least got me out of earshot of Costas and his home improvements. I didn't know it would bring me into the orbit of Ian.

You could quite easily walk past the Red Mill and never know it was there. It's a bizarre little pub, set into a long terrace of Victorian houses, with a polite notice taped on the door asking drinkers to keep the noise down as they leave for the benefit of the neighbors. With its sun trap of a beer garden out the back, bar billiards table, and jukebox packed with albums from seventies dinosaur bands, it attracted what Cameron, the fat, fortysomething landlord, called a "select clientele": mostly bearded real ale drinkers and their aging hippy girlfriends, and the sort of football fan who wanted to discuss the result of the match with the opposition supporters afterward, rather than glass them over it. The only concession Cameron made to the younger drinker was to stock a range of sickly alcopops in Day-Glo colors. But I quickly came to love the atmosphere, the feeling that you'd somehow been invited into the landlord's front room for a pint. Within days, the Red Mill became the stable center of a world which, for me, had been so thoroughly tipped on its axis.

So when Cameron announced that he and Jean, his wife, were taking a couple of months off to visit her elderly, ailing mother in New Zealand, my first thought was to ask how it would affect me. "The brewery'll send a temporary manager, Stella," he told me blithely. "You'll be fine."

And that was how Ian Todd appeared on the scene, and from the moment I saw him, I knew I wouldn't be fine at all.

I turned up for work on the Monday lunchtime, and there he was, bringing a crate of mixers up from the cellar. It was too soon after Martin had walked out on me to be assessing another man sexually, and yet with Ian, I couldn't help it. As his gaze met mine, my pussy clenched with a sudden spasm that was almost painful. It was a reaction no one had garnered from me since Martin. No, make that including Martin.

I don't go for men like Ian, I never have. My ideal is a swarthy, cuddly little bear of a man, just like Martin. Ian was just the opposite: tall and lean, with dishwater blond curls falling to his shoulders, and eyes of a green so pale it was almost colorless. When he spoke, it was with a Liverpool accent, which immediately raised my hackles. It isn't a rational prejudice, but that's the one accent I simply can't stand. It goes all the way back to my old comprehensive school, and the art teacher I had then, Mr. Prior, from somewhere on the Wirral. I was never going to be in the top stream for art—to be honest, most of my efforts gave the impression I just about knew which end of the pencil to draw with—and he was one of those teachers who took great pleasure in ridiculing the less able pupils in a class in front of all the rest. I dropped art as soon as it was no longer compulsory, but even now the sound of those flat Scouse vowels was enough to bring memories of my frequent humiliation at Mr. Prior's hands flooding back.

"You'll be Stella," Ian stated. It wasn't a difficult process of deduction. Cameron only employed two barmaids on a regular basis: me, and an Australian girl called Gill. With her pale, freckled skin, beaky nose, and seventies dress sense she was as far from the Neighbours stereotype of the antipodean beach bunny as it's possible to get, but she had a good rapport with the customers and she worked hard. As did I. Or so I thought till Ian launched into his spiel.

"I don't know quite how much you've been getting away with before," he said, "but I don't stand for any shit. You turn up on time, you don't slope off early because you need to pick up your kids from the babysitter or your period's come on, you don't accept drinks from customers and you make sure the tables in this place are always spotless. No dirty glasses, no full ashtrays. And no slacking. And if you don't like it, tough. Bar staff are ten a penny, and if you don't pull your weight, I can get rid of you like that—" He snapped his fingers contemptuously.

Part of me wanted to tell him to stick his job. Part of me wanted to tell him to stick his fingers in my knickers. What I did was just shrug, and say, "Well, there's nothing like knowing where you stand."

"As long as we understand each other," he said, and turned his back on me to go and fetch another crate of bitter lemon. Oh, I understand you, I thought. You're a shit and you get off on being a shit. It's not big, it's not clever, but I love working here and I'm not going to let you spoil it for me.

Keeping that resolve wasn't easy. It seemed everything I did, everything I said rubbed Ian up the wrong way. Even though I was there from well before my shift started till well after it ended, I always had the feeling he had one eye on his watch as I walked through the door. If he caught Gill and me chatting together, in that first, dead half hour after opening time, he would glare in our direction until one of us went to wipe the already clean tables, or fill bread rolls with cheese and ham and wrap them in clingfilm, ready for the lunchtime rush. We kept smiles plastered to our faces for the benefit of the customers, even when we were calling Ian every name under the sun beneath our breath. And we never, ever gave him the satisfaction of letting him see just how badly he was getting to us.

At the end of the week, he would hand us our pay packets without a word of thanks for our efforts, and I would bite back the urge to tell him not to expect me the following day, since I would be looking for alternative employment. God knew I could find it easily enough: as Ian himself had told me, bar jobs were ten a penny round here. The sensible option would have been to go down to the Internet café on the high street and spend half an hour updating my CV in an attempt to get another management post—something I should have done long before now, in truth—but I was determined that Cameron and Jean would not return from New Zealand to find me gone without an explanation.

What made it more difficult to hold on to my composure was the fact that I was constantly aware of Ian's eyes on me, whether I was stretching to take a shot of whiskey from one of the optics, or bending to load a rack full of dirty glasses into the dishwasher. It was the beginning of August, stiflingly hot, and I was dressing for work in skimpy little vest tops or short, flimsy rayon dresses in a vain attempt to keep cool. As I moved, as Ian watched me, I was sure that he was hoping to catch a glimpse of flesh—a bare, tanned thigh or a small, bra-less breast—through a gap in the loose fabric of my clothes. And sometimes I would catch his gaze, his expression a mixture of disdain and something darker, something greedier.

If Ian had come on to me, I could have coped with it. Years ago, when I had been barely out of my teens and working as an assistant in a shoe shop, I'd had a boss who had taken delight in brushing up against me in the stockroom, "accidentally" touching my breasts and making suggestive remarks. Not knowing how to react and fearful of getting the sack if I spoke to anyone about what was happening, I had stupidly put up with it, even the time he had pressed his hand to the bulge in his regulation black twill trousers and groaned, "You're making it hard for me, Stella." What I should have done was squeeze his balls till he was begging for mercy, P45 or no P45; instead, I put up with his lecherous advances for the next three months, before leaping at the chance to be transferred to the Gillingham branch. I'd already let one man drive me out of my job; perhaps that was why I was so keen it wouldn't happen again. Or perhaps I was just waiting to see whether Ian would finally make the move that proved he wanted me as much as I thought he did, before the tension between us became as unbearable as the heat that assaulted me every time I stepped out of my front door.

Gill didn't seem to have picked up on the situation, but then she was too busy inventing endlessly imaginative ways of torturing Ian, the mildest of which involved stripping him naked, smearing him in honey, and staking him to an anthill. If he'd shown any interest in her, she would have been pretty much oblivious to it anyway, wrapped up as she was in her latest boyfriend, Steve, a burly prop forward for the local rugby team. She described their marathon sex sessions with the same graphic relish she used in her never-ending plans for disposing of Ian—indeed, a couple of them featured the same kitchen utensils. And then Ian would shout across the bar and ask us why we were gossiping when there were customers to be served, and I would go to refill glasses, leaving Gill to wonder aloud just how long it would take Chip and Lemmy, the beer garden rabbits, to nibble Ian to death after she'd shoved carrots in all his orifices.

Although she hated him as much as I did, Gill was openly pleased with the fact that, unlike Cameron, he never let anyone drink in the pub past closing time. Most Friday and Saturday nights, Cameron would have a lock-in with four or five of the regulars, drinking till the small hours of the morning, and he would expect Gill or me to stay behind and join them, at least for an hour or so. Ian wanted us off the premises as soon as possible so he could count the takings, and that suited Gill, who was usually itching to get home to Steve and his amazingly versatile tongue.

I just appreciated the chance to get an extra hour in bed—or at least, that was the plan, until the night I was woken by what sounded like crockery smashing downstairs. Startled, I switched on the light and squinted at the bedside clock. Just gone one in the morning. Through the floorboards, I could hear loud, angry voices. Costas and his wife, arguing. It was a regular occurrence: they would fight, and then they would fuck, the second part of the process being just as noisy as the first. Usually, I would reach for my personal stereo, using music to block out the unwanted sounds of their coupling, but that night I found my hand straying down to part the curls of my bush, a finger slipping inside my pussy to find it moist and wanting. I frigged myself in time to the banging of the bed below me, and in my mind I pictured Ian pressing me down against the mattress, thrusting so hard into me that the breath was forced from my lungs. My fantasies were never this brutal; normally, I imagined myself being stroked and caressed by gentle hands, a soft mouth moving down to tongue the folds of my sex and suck on my clit.

Ian, I was sure, would fuck me without these preliminaries, just yank down my knickers and shove his cock into me, while I moaned and begged him to take me, use me like a cheap whore. I was mouthing the words silently as my fingers moved faster, slithering in the wetness that spilled from my cunt. "Use me, Ian, take me, fuck me." My movements speeded up as the creaking and groaning in the other room got louder and faster, and then Mrs. Costas gave a howl and came, and my own orgasm was triggered by her wild, unearthly cries. In my fantasy, Ian shot his load inside me, then wiped the sticky length of his cock in my hair and walked away.

Needless to say, I didn't mention to Gill that I was fantasizing about being used and abused by Ian Todd; that sort of revelation would not have gone down too well with her. And I certainly couldn't talk about it to the man himself. I mean, how did you tell a bloke you couldn't stand that you got wet at the thought of him holding you down and fucking your brains out? It would have implied I had a personal life, for a start, and Ian never discussed anything even remotely personal with anyone. I didn't even know if he was single: there was no ring on his wedding finger, but for all I knew he could have had anyone waiting for him at home, from a heavily pregnant wife to a garage mechanic called Barry.

We could have gone on like this until he finished his stint as stand-in pub manager, rubbing along together in this unhealthy mix of desire and mutual loathing, but on the last day before Cameron came back, everything went weird. The heat wave was at its height, with that thick heaviness to the air that usually means a storm is on its way. When Ian opened the door of the Red Mill to Gill and me, he was in a truly foul mood, like nothing we had seen from him before. He didn't even acknowledge us as we stepped past him into the already humid interior of the pub.

"Someone's got out of bed the wrong side this morning," I muttered to Gill.

"That guy doesn't have a bed," Gill replied. "He hangs upside down in the wardrobe."

We barely saw Ian during the lunchtime session; the pub was fairly quiet, and he disappeared into the upstairs quarters, muttering about having some paperwork to attend to. Free of his lurking presence, Gill acted like she often did when Cameron was around; flirting outrageously with the customers and putting all her favorite songs on the jukebox. I kept an attentive ear out for Ian's tread on the stairs, but by the time he finally rejoined us, Gill had persuaded the final couple of stragglers that we would be open again in a couple of hours and they could finish their drinking then. He paid us as much attention on the way out as he had coming in.

We opened up again at five; when Ian let us in this time, his hair was wet, as though he'd just come out of the shower. A vision came to me: Ian soaping his lean, naked body as water beat down on him; his hand straying to cradle his cock and start to rub it, steadily—I shook my head: the man would be out of my life in a few hours. It wasn't worth wasting any more of my thoughts on him.

He was still brooding about something, only this time he chose to do it downstairs, glowering at us as he leaned by the till.

"What's eating him?" Gill asked as she passed me, half-a-dozen dirty glasses dangling from her fingers.

"Me, I wish," murmured the small, disloyal voice in the

back of my head. I just shrugged. "Frankly, Gill, I'm way past caring." I'd been asked for a whiskey and green ginger, and I reached past her for the bottle of ginger wine that nestled with all the other rarely used liqueurs at the back of the bar. As my fingers closed round the neck of the bottle, still sticky from the last time it had been used, Gill took a step back from the glass washer and bumped into me. The bottle slithered from my grasp to shatter on the bare floorboards, spattering my sandalled feet and bare shins with liquid.

"Shit!" I exclaimed.

"Don't move, there's glass everywhere," Gill ordered me, hunting under the bar for the dustpan and brush we kept there for incidents such as this.

"You know that's coming out of your wages, don't you?" Ian said. They were the first words he had spoken to me all evening, and something in the tone of his voice, after a day of contemptuous silence, made me snap.

"You've been waiting for this, you bastard," I yelled at him, oblivious to Gill beginning to sweep up the glass fragments and the hapless bloke on the other side of the bar waiting to pay for his drinks. "You've been wanting me to make some mistake so you could bawl me out in front of everyone. Tell me, just what kind of kick do you get out of humiliating your staff? Do you go home at night with a hard-on, knowing you've made someone feel completely worthless?"

The words were falling out of my mouth too fast for me to stop them. Rage was blazing in Ian's eyes, and I knew I'd gone too far, but it felt so good to finally tell him what I thought of him. Gill was getting to her feet, looking at me with something that veered dangerously close to respect, as Ian's hand shot out and caught hold of my wrist.

"That's enough, Stella," was all Ian said, as he yanked me from behind the bar, past a knot of surprised drinkers, so fast my feet were almost pulled from under me. I struggled in his grasp, but he was stronger than he appeared, and that strength alarmed me. I'd intended to provoke some kind of reaction from him, but not this. He dragged me out onto the balcony, slamming the French door behind him, and then he let go of me. It was surprisingly quiet with the noise of the pub muffled; even at the height of summer, the neighbors went to bed early here, ready to rise at six for the following morning's commute. There was enough light for me to see the expression on Ian's face: anger and lust fighting to get the upper hand. Even though there were people sitting less than three feet away on the other side of the door, chatting and laughing over the beat of the music from the jukebox, I suddenly felt vulnerable and very alone.

"Come here," he said, in a low voice that was as threatening as it was sensual. I knew what was about to happen; every moment of our time together had been leading up to this. I needed it—and yet still I feared it. I backed away as far as I could, until I felt the cool wrought iron balustrades of the balcony against the backs of my legs.

"Don't make this difficult for me, Stella," he said. "You want this as much as I do."

And then his hands were on me, lifting me up till I was sitting on the balcony rail, limp as a rag doll in his grip. I knew I shouldn't have been so passive, but arousal was drugging me, making my limbs heavy and fueling my desire to give in.

His mouth met mine, tongue pushing insistently at my lips, forcing them to open and let him in. He tasted of peppermint and lime juice, and I found myself responding, my hands snaking up round his neck, fingers tangling in his messy curls.

He yanked at the neck fastening of my halter top, pulling it apart in one swift movement, baring my breasts to the night air. I broke the kiss in my urge to protest. "Please—someone might come out..."

"And if they do?" Ian's reply was almost a sneer. "Come on, Stella, you know half the blokes in there want to see your tits. Everything you wear shows off those big nipples of yours, you little slut." As he spoke, he took one of my nipples between his fingers, pinching it gently at first, then squeezing it until a moan slipped from my lips, part pleasure, part pain. I could feel my pussy opening against the white cotton of my underwear, the slow pulse between my legs more powerful than that of my heart.

I wanted Ian's fingers in my knickers so badly, but if I asked him to put them there, I knew it would prove me to be the slut he'd already called me. My legs were wrapped round his arse, and I used the backs of my calves to push him a little closer to me, so that his cock was resting against my cunt, hot and vital even through the layers of clothing which separated us.

For a moment, I almost came to my senses, and a voice that didn't sound like mine murmured, "Gill's on her own in there. Won't she start wondering where we've got to?"

"Let her wonder," Ian replied. "She's a big girl, she can look after herself. What are you hoping, Stella, that she might have some problem with a punter and come out here looking for me?"

An image flashed through my mind: Gill's freckled face peering through the French door, in the moment before she framed some question. I knew she wouldn't see too much;

though I was as good as topless, my semi-naked state was obscured by Ian's broad back. And yet a small, shameful part of me hoped she would realize what was happening, and come closer to take a look at my small, uptilted tits with their unmistakably erect nipples. Maybe she would even reach out and pinch one, just as Ian had done—

His next words made even that image seem strangely innocent. "Let's give her something to see if she does come out. Something that'll make her realize just how long you've been starved of cock for."

I heard the metallic rasp of his zip being undone and looked down to see him freeing his cock from his fly. It stood out pale against the black shirt and jeans he wore, long and slender but stiffening as he stroked it. Watching him made me want to reach out and take over, but he was setting the agenda here, so I settled for caressing my own bare breasts.

Ian reached up my skirt and tugged at my knickers. They snagged against my bum and I lifted it slightly, conscious of my precarious position on the balcony rail. The limp white cotton came away in Ian's hand, smelling so strongly of my juices that my cheeks flushed with shame. He let my sodden underwear fall from his grasp, fluttering down like a flag of surrender to land on the picnic table below.

"Oh, Stella, you're so easy," he crooned. "You'll let me do anything, won't you?" As he spoke, his fingers were pushing up into the furnace that was my cunt. His thumb settled on my clit and began to rub. I groaned, no longer caring if anyone heard me.

"Please, Ian, fuck me." The despairing words were so close to all the dirty fantasies I'd woven around him, though I had never pictured myself quite like this, naked except for a couple of rucked-up strips of cloth and my sandals, my legs splayed to give him access to every intimate part of me as I begged for his cock.

He pulled his fingers out of my sex, leaving it gaping and desperately empty. And then I felt a juice-slicked fingertip pressing at the entrance to my arse, and whimpered. Martin had never touched me there—it hadn't been part of our nice, safe sex life—and I wondered how it would feel if Ian decided to thrust up past the tight ring of muscle.

I didn't get the chance to find out. Tired of toying with me, of seeing how willingly I was responding to his depraved little games, he just took hold of his cock and guided it up into my pussy, hard. My cry at being filled to the hilt rang out in the still night air, and I felt sure someone would come out to see what was going on.

My hands were clasped tight round Ian's neck as he began to thrust, my bum slithering on the varnished wood beneath me, even though he was holding my bare cheeks in his hands. With all the tension, all the need that had been building up between us, I was prepared for it to be quick. I wasn't expecting Ian's next words.

"Do you trust me, Stella?" he panted.

"What?" I replied.

"It's a simple question. Do you trust me?"

"I…" The honest answer was no. I didn't trust him; I didn't even like him, and yet he was buried up to the balls in me, fucking me with a purpose and a skill my husband had shown all too rarely over the years of our marriage. "I don't know."

"Well, you're just going to have to." And with that, he reached up a hand and prised my fingers apart. Startled, I found myself falling backward into nothing, and yelped. "It's all right," Ian soothed. "I've got hold of you."

And he had. He was still gripping me tightly, my legs were still wrapped round him and I was still balanced on the balcony rail but my head was pointing down toward the flagstones on which the picnic table stood, thirty feet below. He wouldn't let me drop, I told myself. He couldn't. I felt sick, I felt scared, but most of all I felt horny. The blood was rushing to my head, intensifying every sensation I felt as Ian's hot, thick length continued to pound into me. The situation must have been getting to Ian, too, because his thrusts were faster, less coordinated, and he was grunting with effort.

As Ian's cock jerked inside me and my stomach clenched in the first spasms of orgasm, I let myself go. The rush was like nothing I had known; the blood was singing in my ears and my heels were beating a wild tattoo against the backs of his thighs. That should have been the moment at which the storm broke, fat raindrops beating down on us as we both came. But the thunderclouds continued to hang heavily above us, and as the pleasure began to ebb and reality kicked in, I was left feeling weak and dizzy. I flailed out a hand and grabbed on to the balcony, letting Ian help me to my feet.

As he zipped himself up again and I did my best to rearrange my hopelessly crumpled clothing, I looked for the spark in his eyes that would signify we'd reached some new kind of understanding. I didn't see it. To be honest, I hadn't really expected to.

"So does that pay for the breakages, then?" I asked, as he turned on his heel and stalked back into the bar.

When I turned up for work the next morning, Cameron and Jean were back. They gave no indication that they might have found a stray pair of knickers in the beer garden, so I reckoned Ian must have retrieved them sometime before he'd finally left the pub for good. I wondered if he'd kept them as some kind of warped souvenir, to wank into as he relived our fuck on the balcony. I couldn't ask him: he'd left no note for me, no message of gratitude for the hard work Gill and I had put in for him, no phone number.

I don't know where he's working now, but the brewery owns several pubs in the area, and it's safe to assume he will eventually find himself filling in for the landlord in one of them. I'm not a barmaid at the Red Mill anymore; I finally got my act together and went back into retail management, and now I have a staff of six working beneath me, a respectable, responsible woman once more. And yet on Friday nights I frequent the pubs where Ian might be working, my skirt a little shorter than is decent, and my tight top making it clear I have no bra on beneath it, in the hope that one day I will bump into him. God knows I don't need the aggravation he brings with him, but it seems there's no one else who can quell the heat he left raging in my pussy....

CONSUELA

Alicia Wag

We courted over a checkerboard table for two,
Consuela and I, she licking the brown head of
her chocolate cone, me slurping the pure white
of my cherry vanilla, plucking out the fruity,
burgundy nuggets with my teeth.

Our class—Political Science 101—had been
meeting since the semester began in cold,
frigid, snowy January. It wasn't until March
that I noticed Consuela watching me from
across the lecture hall, her dark eyes peering
up through the flutter of her lashes, her face
shrouded by her long hair, falling like black
silk curtains around her head.

At first I'd only peek back when I knew
she wasn't looking, when she was frantically
scribbling notes, or when she was walking out
of the room, her round ass resplendent in red

corduroys. But after a while I got bolder and met her eyes. She'd cock her lips sideways in a lopsided almost-smile, and her eyes would change, the irises turning darker and shinier, flaring up as if lit from within.

We played like that for weeks, until she was winking at me and blowing kisses. All I could do was smile in return, but that must have told her how much I wanted it. I found myself fantasizing about her; perusing the Internet for pictures of women doing it, looking for information on how to eat pussy, fist, all that stuff I thought lesbians did.

May came. We were getting ready for finals. Consuela came up to me after class. "Hey," she said, tossing her mane behind her shoulder, sleek skin peeking out of the edge of her blue tank top.

"Hey," I whispered.

"Let's go out," she said.

"Now?"

"Yeah," she said. I followed her like a puppy dog. Consuela liked to be in charge. It was to be the basis for our relationship, and something that elicited the most excruciatingly wonderful orgasms I'd ever had, while eventually getting tiresome and frustrating. But I'm getting ahead of myself.

That warm day in May, Consuela led me to the ice cream shop, where she ordered a chocolate cone for herself and a cherry vanilla one for me. She carried both to a table and nodded at the chair I was to use. I parked my hot ass down. Consuela took the seat across from me. When she handed me my cone, I was salivating.

I held it, waiting for her to tell me what to do. I was already with the program, without even knowing what the program was. Consuela told me later I was a natural, whispered it wetly into my ear, biting vigorously on my earlobe, after fucking my brains out with the biggest dildo she could find.

She rolled out her tongue first, showing it to me. Then she brought the cold, wet ice cream to it. Once she had it good and licked, she reached across the table and shoved it in my mouth, hard, so that I had to bite it to keep it from choking me. I laughed into the ice cream. I was loving it, even the shock of the cold in my mouth and the pain in my teeth.

We went to the ice cream parlor after class for the next three weeks. I practiced every technique I could on those cones, getting ready. A lot of them I copied from Consuela.

In the fourth week, Consuela's bare foot found my pussy under the table. I was wearing a sundress with no underwear, as Consuela had instructed me to do the week before. I felt the ball of her foot sink into the warm wet of my cunt, rubbing all over. I closed my eyes and tried not to moan.

"Keep licking," Consuela ordered, and I went back to my ice cream cone, pretending it was Consuela's cunt, sucking and mouthing while her toes tickled my pussy. Her big toe found my hole, and I spread my legs wider to receive it, moving my ass back and forth gently on the chair. She fucked me like that for a minute, then brought her toes up to my clit, pressing hard in circular motions. I came in about a second. As I sat at the little checkerboard table panting, Consuela's hand, the one holding her cone, reached underneath and planted the rounded, well-licked, freezing head of chocolate ice cream onto my steaming, juiced pussy.

I cried out so loudly the only two other people in the shop turned to look. Consuela laughed, and so did I.

It definitely wasn't the last time she surprised me.

I took longer than Consuela did to finish our final, but when I entered the hallway, I found her waiting, leaning against the graffitied wall.

She made a cradle with her left elbow and put her books in it, while the index finger of her right hand curled around a belt loop in my jean shorts. She pulled me two blocks off campus to her apartment, a messy studio on the fourth floor. When we walked into the building, she made me go first, and alternated between pushing me up the stairs and squeezing and twisting my buttcheeks in her hand.

Her door was unlocked. Consuela dropped her books on the counter in the kitchenette. I put mine on a chair, and turned to look at the king-size futon that dominated the room. It was on the floor, covered with red satiny sheets, littered with glittery, sequined pillows of black and royal blue and mustard yellow, fraying tassels hanging from their corners. An upside-down wooden crate served as the night table, covered with an embroidered cloth. On it were a glass lamp, lord knows how many harnesses tangled up with each other, two tubes and one bottle of lube, and some other things I couldn't identify.

Consuela went into the kitchen and lifted something out of a pot. When she came back out, I saw that it was a jet black dildo: a slightly curved, thick cock with a generous head. She smiled at me and kissed its head, then pointed to the bed. "Get on it," she said. "On your knees." I took off my sandals and went to the middle of the futon, which was much cushier than I expected. The satin felt smooth and luxurious under my bare knees. "Watch me," said Consuela. "Don't take your eyes off me."

She put the base of the dildo between her teeth and held it there while she pulled both straps of her loose turquoise tank dress down until it was hanging on her like a skirt. Her breasts were big and firm, round like the rest of her, their brown middles dark with desire, the nipples as hard and erect as the cock in her mouth. She wiggled her hips until the dress fell in a pile at her feet. She was already wearing a harness, black leather wrapped around her hips, just underneath the luscious mound of her belly, her bush as shiny and black as her hair. It became the black cock's bush as she took it out of her mouth, lowered it down with her hands, and strapped it on. She walked to the night table, ripped open a condom, and rolled it onto the dildo. She laughed and thrust it back and forth at me a few times, then said, "Strip, Kathy."

I undid my shorts, pulled them off, and lifted my tank top over my head. I was in such a tizzy it got stuck around my neck, and I fiddled with it frantically for a few seconds before getting it all the way off. Consuela was coming toward me, her gorgeous lips that I hadn't yet kissed, her delicious tits that I wanted to suck, her big black cock that was going to have its way with me. Somewhere underneath it all was the pussy I had been imagining.

As she walked, her hand wrapped around the dildo, fondling it, I thought about how I looked to her. I was nothing special. Where she had long, black, phenomenal hair, mine was mousy brown, short enough to show off the multiple piercings along the edges of my ears. Where her body was voluptuous and sexy, mine was thin and angular, with small boobs, the kind people like to refer to as perky. They were pink, though, and I found out later Consuela liked that, the way she liked my boniness, my pale skin, and especially my lack of pussy hair, which I'd been shaving since I discovered how much better cocks and tongues and fingers felt without it.

Consuela kept coming until the dildo was hitting me in the face. She whapped one cheek, then the other, then pushed me over with her knees. I lay on my back, my legs outspread, my mouth and my pussy watering. She put one foot on my belly, and reached to the side of the futon, where she found a pair of black leather studded bracelets held together by a silver chain.

Once she had them she kneeled over me, the cock resting happily in the space between my tits, grabbed my hands, and put one bracelet on, then the other. Once I was good and cuffed, I lay back, stretching my arms over my head and my legs out long and wide. Consuela kneeled beside me and whispered in my ear. "Are you ready for Mama?" she asked.

"Mmmmm," I murmured, completely psyched about the luxury of being helplessly fucked.

"Mama's going to take care of you," Consuela whispered, licking my ear, running her tongue along the studs and hoops. She licked along my cheek to my mouth, her fleshy, tawny lips opening my thinner, pinker ones, kissing me long and deep, fucking my mouth with her tongue, sucking and biting my bottom lip. I started to tongue her back, but she pulled away and smacked my face. "Bad girl," she said. "Don't do that without permission." I smiled and she smacked me again. Her tits were hanging low, dangling against my chin, driving me nuts. "Tell Mama you're sorry."

"I'm sorry, Mama," I said, restraining myself from lifting my head and trying to nibble on one of her tits.

"That's a good girl," said Consuela, taking my nipples between her fingers, pinching and twisting. I moaned and she did it harder. "Does it hurt?" she asked.

"Yes," I whispered.

"Does it hurt good?"

"It hurts fucking great," I said, and moaned louder as she started sucking my nipples, nursing them with her teeth and lips and tongue until my whole body was hot and buzzing. She put her hand around my pussy, tickling my lips and clit with her long red fingernails. I moved my hips up and down, opened my legs wider, lifted my ass to open my cunt as far as it would go, let her swallow it up. She licked the smooth skin around my clit and lips until I thought I'd die from anticipation. Then the darting tip of her tongue went inside me, and she sucked until I came in her open mouth.

She kept her mouth there for a minute, letting my cunt throb in it, then she got back onto her knees and grabbed a tube of lube. She juiced up the dildo and kneeled between my legs, grabbing my hips hard and pulling my ass and pussy up and into her, onto the black cock, thrusting so deeply I felt it all the way to my belly. She fucked me hard for a long time, bouncing me against her so fast I could feel my tits shake wildly. My first time with a woman, and I was getting fucked with a cock. It had been a long time since I'd gotten anything, but this was different than a flesh and blood dick. Consuela held my hips hard, her eyes rolled back in her head, lovely. It occurred to me that the dick was fucking her, too, that we were connected by it, that it was pleasuring both of us, an instrument of our mutual desire, the energy of our wanting fueling it, making it alive.

Consuela didn't cry out, but I saw her shudder, her body shaking inwardly into orgasm, and my heart melted. Then she turned me over, grabbing my asscheeks in her fists, slapping them with her hands while she pumped me from behind.

After, she lay beside me, gently stroking my tits and my

belly and my bald pussy for a few minutes, smiling. Within that calm, she unbuckled her harness, tossed it and the dick aside, freed me from the cuffs, and hugged me close. I put one of my hands on her breast, squeezed it and played with it just the way I wanted to. I knew she wasn't Mama now, just Consuela, the hot, lovely, Consuela I'd been imagining for so long.

I laid her down on the red satin, among all the wet spots my come and hers had made, and spread her open to see her luscious pussy, brown along the edges, shining and pink and swollen inside, and I ate her like a cherry vanilla ice cream cone, until every drop, every crumb was finished.

The semester was over. I had a summer job interning at a newspaper. Consuela was working for a congressional candidate. We met for lunch, chatted about our work, our majors, our childhoods. Nights we spent on red satin, fucking.

After two weeks of heaven, Consuela told me about Leif. "Leif's coming home tomorrow."

"Who's Leif?" I asked sleepily, twirling the soft coils of her bush around my fingers.

"My boyfriend. He's been away, studying overseas. He's coming back tomorrow."

I was only in a little bit of shock. "What does that mean?" I asked.

"Don't worry, Kathy," she whispered, reaching for the cuffs. "You're going to love him."

Leif arrived in town on a Tuesday. Consuela informed me that she'd need time with him alone, and she'd call me when she was ready. I protested, not sure I could bear being without her for very long. She agreed to have lunch with me on Thursday.

We met at a deli, where Consuela ordered an egg salad plate, and I had a Reuben with fries. After proceeding through the line, grabbing Diet Cokes and napkins and silverware, we picked a corner table and sat down.

"How's work?" asked Consuela.

"Fine," I said. "The tax override was voted down. That's what I wrote about today."

"Sounds thrilling," said Consuela. "I went to a dinner with important people last night."

"What did you wear?" I teased, running my toes along her shin.

"Red," said Consuela. "Leif's favorite." I froze and took a deep breath. Consuela put her hand on mine. "Don't be jealous, Kathy. I love you both."

"Then why aren't you seeing me?"

She laughed. "You're a hungry, naughty girl, Kathy." Consuela chewed on a piece of celery. "Friday. We'll go out to dinner."

"You and me?" I asked, favoring denial over reality.

"And Leif," said Consuela. "We'll see how it goes, and take it from there."

"Okay," I said, even though it didn't feel one bit okay.

But at that point, I'd have done anything for Consuela.

She picked Italian, and I ordered lasagna to avoid the awkwardness of spaghetti. It didn't work, entirely. There was a side of pasta, a pile of smooth noodles covered by shimmering red sauce and salty cheese.

Consuela had no inhibitions about spaghetti or anything

else. She ordered fettucini Alfredo, and ate it one noodle at a time, just barely using her fork, mostly using her mouth like a vacuum cleaner. She was remarkable, doing it with total finesse.

I watched her, enjoying the white sauce that spilled onto and around her lips, the way she licked them clean with her tongue. I was also avoiding Leif, who turned out to be the quiet, intellectual type, nothing like I'd imagined.

Yes, I had tried to imagine him. For the painful days without Consuela, I tried to think about what I knew she was planning. What was it about a three-way that terrified me? I didn't know, I only knew that I would do it if Consuela wanted me to, but I'd be clinging to her all the while, and whatever I gave to Leif would be for her.

"Talk to her, Leif," said Consuela.

He smiled mildly, showing off his straight teeth, lifting his cup of tea to his mouth and sipping. "Yes, love," he said with the slightest hint of an accent. He turned to me. "Kathy, I'm afraid we're both shy."

"She's not shy," Consuela said, and I blushed.

I forced myself to talk. "So you're in law school?"

He shifted in his seat, made himself that much closer to me. "Mmm," he said. "Yes." He'd been drinking dark German beer all night, and I could smell the way it lingered on his breath.

I sipped my Campari with lime. It warmed my belly, making me relax and sink lower in my seat as Consuela took over the chatting. She was remarkably generous, lavishing attention on Leif and me virtually equally, which made me relax even more. I started to really look at Leif, listen to his deep, resonant, Scandinavian voice speak in measured, calm tones.

He was extremely mellow, highly articulate, and obviously intelligent. I checked out his large, sinewy hands, with long, graceful fingers and rounded fingertips. Broad shoulders. Strong. No hair peeking from the open top buttons of his preppy button-down shirt. I guessed he was smooth, and perfect, like a marble statue.

After dinner we walked to the Common, sitting on one park bench after another, taking turns being in the middle. Consuela took the first turn, putting her arms around both of us, pulling us in. The park was dark and quiet, moonlight mixing with the occasional streetlamp, glowing in the summer night. She kissed me first, and I rejoiced inside. Then she kissed Leif, and then put one hand behind my head, and the other behind Leif's, drawing the two heads together, mine and Leif's, until his barely scented beer breath met mine, bitter with Campari, sour with lime, sweet with gelato, and we kissed, our lips finding each other slowly, tentatively, licking and sucking with our teeth and tongues, while Consuela watched, sighing deeply.

By the time we hit the fourth bench, we were all kissing at the same time, and finding each other's erect nipples, hard cock, and swollen pussies through our clothes, and Consuela said, "Let's go." And of course, I did.

We went to Leif's, a luxury two-bedroom in a downtown high-rise. The place was spotless. Clean, orderly, comforting. Leif pulled back the spread on the round king-size bed with clean cotton sheets. Outside the huge picture window, city lights twinkled. I walked up to the sheet of glass and stared into the view, Consuela behind me, pulling off my shorts and shirt. As I looked into the night, watched it unfold far into the distance, I felt like we were flying above the whole world.

When I turned around Consuela and Leif were already naked. He was as well put together as his home, as clean, as inviting, and, as I'd guessed, as perfect. His cock stood straight up, the head peeking out of his foreskin, and I felt a thrill seeing that he was uncut. He was watching me, too, and I felt a stab of self-consciousness, comparing myself with Consuela's earthy beauty. But he was smiling, a different kind of smile than he'd used in the restaurant, where he'd been all civilized and reserved.

"On the bed, Kathy," said Consuela. "With your back against the headboard." I climbed on the circular mattress, leaned against the oak headboard, opened my legs to show them both my pussy. Consuela had Leif's cock in her hand, moving back and forth so his dick fully emerged from the foreskin. She was whispering in his ear, mumblings I couldn't understand. I had a vague feeling of not liking that, but I ignored it, transfixed by the sight of Consuela pleasuring Leif with her hand, kissing his mouth and his ear. Despite any jealousy I might have, it was a beautiful sight, watching the woman I'd fallen so hard for with a man I knew she loved.

She let go of his cock, led him to the bed where I was waiting. She leaned her face into my cunt, licking and sucking all the ways she knew I liked. I opened as wide as I could, but I never felt like I could make myself as open as I wanted to be, open enough for Consuela to fall inside me. Leif's hand squeezed mine and I squeezed back as Consuela's mouth took me in. He whispered to Consuela, encouraging her, "Yes, love, that's right love, that's beautiful, love." His words echoed in my head—yes, love, good, beautiful, now—until my body shook and pulsed and I lay back, spent and happy.

Consuela kneeled beside Leif and kissed him, giving my taste to his mouth. After a moment she pulled back and said, "She's yours now." He stood up and she slapped his ass. "Go," she said, like she was desperate, like she had been waiting a long time for this moment of watching Leif fuck me.

He took me the way she had the first time, pulling me up by the hips and thrusting hard and deep. Consuela pulled a dildo out of her bag and fucked herself while we fucked. Leif watched her, jerking up and down on the dildo until she came, crying out louder than I'd ever heard her. Then Leif pulled out of me and climbed off the bed, pulling Consuela's head toward him so she could take him in her mouth.

I watched her lick my juices off his hard cock, take the whole length of it in and out, suck it until his ass and hips stiffened and he came, Consuela's mouth holding the whole of him until he finished.

They both climbed in bed with me, and we cuddled, Leif and I, with Consuela, the major object of our affections, in between us.

A SPANKING GOOD TIME

Eva Hore

We'd only been married a short time and I was still adjusting to having moved into Brian's apartment. Things were going reasonably well. Sex was great and we had a happy and open relationship. The only problem was that his boss was always ringing up to get him to work on weekends and today was no exception.

"Why can't he ring someone else?" I pouted.

"He has. I told you, Melissa, no one else is available," Brian said.

"It's not fair," I moaned. "I wanted us to do something special tonight."

"We will. I won't be long, I promise," he said, kissing me on the top of my head. "Why don't you go through my videos and see what takes your fancy. Don't pick any with the red labels, okay? There's a bottle of wine in the fridge. I'll pick up Chinese on the way home."

"Sure, that'll be so much fun," I said sarcastically.

I found a tape marked with a red label titled, *A Spanking Good Time* and slotted it into the VCR. I poured a glass of wine and settled back to watch what I assumed would be a porno. I knew he had them and it didn't bother me that he did. Most guys liked watching porn and I was a liberated woman so why shouldn't I?

I hit the play button, spluttering my drink as I witnessed Brian, starring in what looked like a homemade porno.

"Come here, baby, so I can give you what you need. Come on, you know you love it," he was saying.

"No, I don't want to," the woman said, crossing her long legs.

"Come here," he demanded.

"No," she said, swinging her foot around.

"Mary, do as you are told," he said more firmly.

She giggled, "No!"

A wave of jealously washed over me.

"Good. Look at the video camera, really work it," he said, directing her. "Come over here like I asked?"

She rose slowly, smoothing down her skirt, and sashayed over to stand in front of him, her hands folded, lips slightly open, pouting at him.

"You know I have to punish you, don't you?"

She nodded her head.

"You always have to be punished when you disobey me, don't you?"

Giggling, she bent over his knees. He pulled up her skirt.

She was wearing white panties; full panties like you did when you went to school.

His hands roamed over them, fingers sliding underneath the gusset.

"Hmm," she sighed.

He slapped her lightly. She said nothing. She just lay there.

"You've been a bad, bad girl," he said.

Now he slapped her harder.

"Oww!" she cried.

"That's what happens when you don't do as you're told," Brian said.

"You're hurting me," she whined. "Please stop."

Brian acted as though he didn't hear her and kept on hitting her, slapping his hand backward and forward, ignoring her pleas.

"That's hurting," she said, pouting her lips as she looked over at the camera.

"It's supposed to hurt, Mary," Brian said, lifting her skirt higher, pulling her panties down and exposing her red cheeks.

I couldn't believe what I was watching. I knew he was kinky, but this... I didn't know why, but anger surged through me. Now I knew why he demanded I not watch the ones with red labels.

I studied him closely, looking for changes in his appearance. When had this film been made? He did look younger, his hair longer and his body more toned than it had been when we'd first met. It better be years old or all hell would break loose.

He rubbed his hands over her bum, caressing it with circular motions, running his finger down the crack, over her hole.

He kneaded the cheeks, opening them, inspecting her, before sliding his finger further toward her pussy.

I subconsciously clenched my own cheeks. That was something we hadn't done. I didn't realize he was into this sort of thing.

She moved her hands, trying to cover herself. He smacked them away. She squirmed trying to get up, but he held her down.

"You're hurting me!"

"You shouldn't have put your hands there. You know the rules. Now I'll have to spank you with the ruler."

Rules! What rules? How many times had he done this to her?

"I think I've had enough," she said, turning her head to speak to him, although I did notice her bum seemed to rise higher.

"What's the rule on talking?"

"I can't remember," she whined.

"Second rule is no talking. Now I'm going to have to spank you harder."

I could see her bum getting even redder as he hit her with the ruler. He expertly slipped her panties down to her ankles, sliding them off one leg to leave them dangling on the other. With his free hand he pushed her legs apart, giving himself a nice view of her pussy.

Oh, she was enjoying this all right.

"Please don't," she said, trying to pull her legs back together.

"I said no talking, Mary. You like being a bad girl, don't you?" he said, forcing her legs wide open.

"No, I don't," she said in a pathetic voice.

Brian ignored her, and alternated the spanking, giving her one stroke with the ruler, then rubbing his hand over her bum and giving her a sharp slap with his hand. Occasionally, he'd touch her pussy and I watched her bum rise seductively, encouraging him for more.

Bitch! I don't know why but I was mad at both of them. What a performance they were putting on. How could she allow him to videotape her like this? Acting out a fantasy was one thing but to put it on tape for others to see, well that just wasn't on.

"Stop it. You're hitting too hard," she begged.

"Quiet!" he commanded, hitting her pussy. "Not another word."

Mary stopped complaining and began moaning, making whimpering noises. The smack on her pussy had her lifting her bum even higher, wiggling it in front of him, begging him to do it again.

"I think you're enjoying this, Mary," Brian said, chuckling. "Do you think I need to punish you some more?"

"Yes, please," she giggled.

"Stand for me," he said, smoothing her skirt over her naked bum. "How about you take off your skirt for me?"

She was standing with her back to him and I watched as she looked over her shoulder and ran her tongue over her top lip as she slipped off her skirt. She kicked up her other leg, discarding her panties, and stood there, naked from the waist down. He rubbed his hands over her body, lingering over the welts that had formed on her cheeks before turning her around.

When she was facing him again he caressed her stomach, travelling slowly downward until he touched her pubic hair.

I downed the rest of my drink, feeling the alcohol heat up my stomach like this video was heating up my pussy.

"You've got lovely red hair, haven't you? Oh, and a little further down there's some on your pussy. Hmm, it's a nice pussy isn't it? Come and let me see the rest of you," he said, moving his hands under her blouse.

She undid each button, teasing him as she went, pouting her lips and looking up at him through her lashes. Her blouse dropped to the floor and she stood there in only a white bra.

She certainly wasn't pretending not to like what he was doing now, was she?

Brian ran his fingers over the lace on the bra and forced her breasts up so they hung out over the top.

I grabbed the remote and hit *pause*. I quickly went into the kitchen to refill my glass, then hurried back and started it up again. I wanted to make sure I saw it all before Brian came home.

"You've got magnificent breasts," he was saying, giving the nipples a quick suck.

I had to admit she did. She also had a great body and knew it.

Giggling, she ran her hands down her stomach and over her mound to touch her pussy. Separating the lips she slid a finger inside. She leaned back against the desk, opening her legs, so her pussy was more visible for him while she fingered herself.

He knelt down, running his tongue over her pussy and giving her a long lick.

"You like being a good girl now, don't you?" he said unclipping her bra and allowing it to fall to the floor. She was naked except for her high-heeled shoes.

"Yes, I like being good," she said.

"And you like being spanked good and proper, don't you?"

"Oh yes," she breathed.

"Lean over the desk so I can spank you some more."

She didn't hesitate. She leaned on the desk with her bum twitching in the air, her feet slightly apart. She shook her hair seductively, allowing it to caress her face before looking long and hard into the camera. I pulled back instinctively. It was as though she knew I was there, watching.

I wondered what it would feel like to have Brian do that to me. To videotape me in the nude. Would it turn him on? Would he watch it when I wasn't home? Would he show his friends?

That thought startled me. I wondered if he'd had nights over here with his mates. If they sat around drinking and watching these sort of tapes. What did they do? Did they pull at their cocks, relieve themselves in front of each other, or what? I knew I was feeling horny so I could only imagine how guys must feel when they see this sort of thing, and with them it was hard to hide.

Back on-screen, Brian stood and out of his drawer he produced a small whip. It looked like it was made of suede. Gently he lashed her.

"Oh no, don't, please don't!" she complained.

She didn't sound too convincing to me.

Smirking, Brian spread her legs wider so he could see her pussy. He bent down, gave it a little lick and began to whip a bit harder. She put her hands behind, to protect herself again.

"Didn't I tell you not to do that?"

"You're hurting me."

"Do you like being disobedient?"

"No, I don't. You're hurting me I said."

"It's supposed to hurt. You like me spanking you, don't you?"

"No, I don't," she insisted.

"Yes, you do. I can see your pussy, I can see your juices oozing out over your lips," he said, rubbing his hand over it. "Oh yes. You are enjoying this, aren't you Mary?"

"No, I'm not."

"Well that's not what your pussy's telling me," he said, slipping in his finger. "Oh, yeah, that's juicy. You love it."

She grabbed his hand, holding it there. Her bum was moving toward his crotch as he withdrew his fingers, to smear her juices over her crack. I watched as he fell to his knees, lowering his head to lick the welts. He ran his tongue over them, then her hole, stopping just before her pussy.

I was sitting on the edge of my seat. My breasts were tingling, my pussy throbbing.

She was up on her elbows now, pulling at her breasts, teasing the nipples to make them erect, pushing her bum into Brian's face, trying to get him to put his tongue inside her.

"That's one hot bum," he said laughing.

He took the handle of the whip, probed her pussy with it. She wiggled her bum around and he held on to her, pushing the handle in and out. He moved back out of the way and I watched fascinated as he now inched it into her hole, slowly probing but not hurting.

I was unable to tear my eyes away from this spectacle. I could see the bulge in Brian's trousers. I wondered how much longer they were going to do this and if he was going to fuck her as well.

He told her to stand, helping her up on the desk, bending her over so her pussy was level with his face. She squealed with delight as he alternated between smacking her and giving her pussy a long lick, from her clit all the way up to her hole. It was driving her wild. She was gyrating her pussy into his face, encouraging him for more.

With his free hand he undid his trousers and they fell to his ankles. He stood there looking ridiculous with his cock hanging out. He covered her pussy with his mouth, nuzzling and sucking as he removed his shirt. Now they were both naked.

My own pussy was swelling and I moved uncomfortably on the couch. I was shocked to see Brian naked. There was something not right about watching your husband and another woman, even if it was an old tape, and it had better be.

Grabbing her hips he pulled her back over the edge of the desk and pushed her roughly, facedown, onto it. Papers and pencils flew onto the floor. Her breasts squashed against the desk. He held her firmly in this position, his cock resting between her cheeks. He began smacking her thighs again and I could see how much redder her bum was. It looked like he'd broken the skin but she seemed oblivious to it. She was really getting off and Brian was in his element.

He loved to be in control.

"Spread your legs, baby," he said.

She didn't hesitate.

He parted her cheeks, rubbing his cock over her hole and pussy. He was wetting his cock, teasing her pussy by just putting it in a fraction and then pulling back, just like he did with me.

"Fuck me. Oh please, fuck me," she begged.

I squirmed on the couch; my pussy was throbbing, wanting

some attention. I crossed my legs, but that only made it pulsate more.

He continued to tease her with his cock, rubbing it up and down her slit, and she was trying desperately to grab it and put it inside her.

He pulled back away from her, left her on her own on the desk and walked around her, eyeing her. He pulled his cock, aiming it toward her, and she moved forward, her tongue stretching out, trying to lick the knob. He kept her at bay, pumping the shaft, allowing pre-come to dribble out, and now she lunged for his cock, pulling him closer to devour in her mouth.

"Yes. Oh god, yes," she mumbled, wild for him, gobbling at his cock like someone starved for food.

He pumped himself into her mouth and I could see by his face he was on the verge of coming. He pulled himself out, her saliva dripping on the desk as he moved back behind her.

He grabbed her hips firmly, pulling her hard toward him and plunged his cock straight into her pussy, the force of it throwing her forward on the desk. He thrust in deeper and harder, making her scream and cry out for more. The desk was shifting under the pounding he was giving her. Sweat was pouring off him, dripping onto her back.

"Quickly," he demanded, frantically trying to calm himself down. "Turn around and sit on the desk with your legs open wide."

From this angle I could see her pussy completely. They knew how to work the camera and I fleetingly wondered if they'd acted out any other scenarios and if they were around the house somewhere just waiting for me to find. I downed the rest of my drink, wanting more but not wanting to miss a thing as she sat with her legs hanging over the side of the desk, her breasts heaving.

I moved my hand down inside my panties to my pussy. It was nice and wet and I slipped a finger in, then another as I opened my thighs and leaned back on the couch to locate my clit. It was already hard. I rubbed it quickly, enjoying the sensation.

"Now open your mouth. Wider," he commanded, as he pushed his cock in.

This threw her into a frenzy. She squirmed and bucked on that desk as he rammed his fingers inside her, finger-fucking her while she sucked his cock, loudly slurping and choking on it as he pushed himself further into her mouth.

I quickly pulled my panties down, as they were constricting my hand, and rubbed my clit harder. I finger-fucked myself, reaching a high I hadn't felt for a long time, as I watched them.

Then he turned her around, slamming her facedown on the desk again, grabbing both legs, pulling them wide apart and ramming his cock into her hole. She was delirious with passion, grabbing at his arse, pulling him into her, matching his thrusts as he plunged into her over and over.

I frantically rubbed myself, my fingers massaging my clit, bringing me to a powerful orgasm.

Finally, he pulled his cock out of her and sprayed his come over her face and breasts. She loved it. I watched her smear it into her mouth, licking and sucking it off her fingers.

The film panned out and I pulled my panties up, covering my saturated pussy, and lay completely back against the couch, exhausted.

"Having fun?" Brian asked, interrupting my thoughts.

I jumped, embarrassed at having been caught out. I realized from his casual stance he'd been watching me for some time.

"Me...er...having fun? What about you?" I spluttered, angrily turning on him.

"What are you mad at me for?" he asked. "I told you not to watch the ones with red labels."

"When did you make this movie?" I demanded.

"Ages ago. There's nothing wrong with having it. It's not like I did it yesterday. It was years ago, before I even knew you."

"That's not the point. You should have destroyed it when we met," I said angrily.

"No, you shouldn't have watched it. You do look sexy when you're mad, Melissa," he said coming close to me. "I'll bet your pussy's on fire."

It was, but I wasn't going to tell him that.

"I demand you throw it away. It's disgusting," I said, wild with indignation.

"Is it now?" he said, as he grabbed the back of my head with one hand, pulling me into his body.

I tried to pull back, but he held me even tighter, breathing into my ear as he kissed my neck. I gasped when I felt his hand lift my skirt. He tore off my panties, the elastic leaving a stinging sensation.

"Don't," I said only halfheartedly.

"Don't! That's not what your pussy's saying. I was watching you enjoy yourself. I think you might enjoy a spanking too for..."

"What? I would not," I said, only moderately upset, as I felt a stirring deep inside me.

He pushed me back onto the couch and I tried to fight him

off. We wrestled together and he tore the buttons on my shirt. I gasped as his hands pulled open my shirt and he lunged at my breasts, his fingers fumbling as he ripped the cups apart.

I'd never seen him so forceful. He was usually so considerate and sweet. I liked him like this. Aggressive and demanding as he squeezed one breast while his mouth smothered the other.

I was panting hard as he grabbed both of my hands and held them over my head. His eyes were wild as his other hand pushed my legs apart and he groped for his cock, rubbing my pussy with it before he plunged it inside me.

My body betrayed me by allowing his cock to slip in so easily. I was swimming with juices. Brian looked down at me, a smile crossing his handsome face.

Bastard. He knew me so well.

Still holding me firmly, he pushed deeper inside me, bringing me to a wonderful orgasm. My eyes closed in ecstasy only to quickly fly open as I felt the sharp sting of pain when he slapped me hard on the thigh.

"Stop it!" I demanded. "Don't, Brian. I don't like it," I said, as he slapped me again.

"Yes you do. Your pussy's getting much wetter now. Come on, admit it?"

"I don't," I said, only halfheartedly. I was enjoying it, but I didn't want Brian to know. Slapping me on the thigh with his open hand was one thing, whipping me was definitely out of the question.

My pussy was on fire. With each slap, I felt myself building to a mind-shattering orgasm. My juices flowed out of me, over his cock and into his pubic hair. I couldn't stop. I was wild with desire.

"Oh, Brian," I begged. "Please don't stop. Don't stop."

I couldn't help myself, couldn't stop myself from saying it. God I wanted it, wanted it bad.

He laughed. Letting go of my hands he rolled us off the couch and onto the floor with me on top of him. Slipping straight in, his cock was like a gun, honing in on its target and hitting its mark. I was sitting astride his amazing cock rocking back and forth as though riding a horse. I loved this position and began to ride him harder and harder.

His hands were on my cheeks, pulling them apart, gently running the tips of his fingers around my hole, tickling it. I was remembering how he'd done it on the video and it was turning me on even more. I imagined someone watching us, watching me, as the light slaps, in between caresses, became louder.

My pussy was throbbing like never before. The stinging sensation of pain turned into exquisite torture, driving me out of my mind. I couldn't stop coming. I could think of nothing else but what he was doing. As he finally came I collapsed on top of him, my breathing labored.

"Oh, god, Brian. That was amazing," I said, smothering his face with kisses.

"I told you you'd enjoy it," he said, chuckling. "Come on, admit it?"

"Well, maybe just a little. But I don't want you to do it again, okay?"

"Sure," he said smugly, stroking my hair.

I did want to do it again, boy did I, but I wasn't going to tell him that. I'd wait until the time was right, then I'd surprise him with a small whip of my own. Maybe I could find out where this Mary woman lived and she could join me. We could tie him up, see how much he liked it. Have him at our mercy.

With those pleasant thoughts running through my mind I drifted off into a light sleep, dreaming about being tied up and at the mercy of many men. Of being laid out on a bed, spread-eagled and naked. My pussy, hole, and tits being attacked, fingered, sucked, and licked by all the men with Brian looking on.

With a smile on my lips I fell into an exhausted slumber.

BUSTED

Jordana Winters

"Shit!"

Busted for speeding—fantastic—just what she needed. Elena glanced again in the rearview mirror. There had been no movement from the police car in the few minutes she'd been waiting. What the hell was taking so long?

She opened her glove compartment and rifled through her papers, searching for her insurance.

She jumped at the loud knock on the window.

"Hi," Elena said, as she rolled down the window, playing sweet. She hoped the cop was male, very cute, and easily influenced by a pretty face.

The flashlight shining directly into her eyes made it impossible to see if it was a man or woman.

"Get out of the car," his voice boomed, commanding her attention.

"What?"

"Get out of the car."

She glanced again in the rearview. It certainly looked like a police car—roof lights flashing, the whole bit. Still, she was a lone woman on the side of the highway. Like hell she was getting out.

"Sorry. I'm not comfortable with that. How do I know you're really a cop?" she asked, squinting, putting her hand up to block the light.

"I'm not telling you again. Get out of the car," he repeated, bending down so she could see his face.

"Jackson? Jesus! You had me going," she smiled, instantly relieved, letting her arm rest on the open window.

He pulled the door open, catching her by surprise, making her move her arm or she'd have tumbled out.

"Out of the car please ma'am."

She released herself from her seat belt and climbed out, taking him all in. It was the first time she'd seen him in his uniform, and it wasn't disappointing.

"Nice," she purred, biting into her lower lip.

With Jackson, she had broken all her rules. That she had agreed to meet, after talking to him for less than a week through an online dating site, had taken even her by surprise. His picture. Holy Christ. He was hot. Hot, hot. His voice, deep yet relaxed, had her trembling before he'd gotten his first ten words out.

So, she'd ended up at his place, in his bed, because crashing on his conveniently too-small couch hadn't been "acceptable."

Elena had seen two uniform shirts hanging side by side when she'd hung up her coat. His cop boots lay on the closet floor. Sweet Jesus. Finally—her long sought-after cop.

Jackson, coming to bed in his Calvin Kleins and tight black T-shirt, alluringly scented in Dolce & Gabbana, had sealed the deal. All her good-girl rules had ceased to exist. Him curling up behind her, his body warm and tight against hers, had felt deliciously romantic and deliciously sinful at the same time.

Following that was a massage, him pulling her hair and kissing her neck. Telling him to stop had seemed her only option. A minute longer and she'd have been unable to stop herself. So they'd snuggled, her lying in the crook of his shoulder, alternating featherlike strokes with her fingertips over his belly, then with her nails, which evoked deep groans from him. Jackson's body was exquisite—chiseled, hairless, and soft as silk. Her hand had strayed further, grazing over his hard-on that strained against his boxers. She'd stopped herself again, feigned being tired and rolled over to sleep. She'd barely slept a wink.

They'd fucked on their second date. By that point she had little choice. Her expectations of how good he was going to be hadn't fallen short. He fucked hard and he fucked rough—a perfect combination as far as she was concerned.

The strangeness of the conversation they'd had just ten minutes earlier was now explained. She'd been nearly out the door when the phone rang. He'd asked her where she was going and which road she was taking. At the time she'd thought it odd. Now, it all made sense.

He stood before her, dressed in the full uniform, Kevlar

vest, gun jutting off the side of his belt, cop boots, cop pants, ass tight and delicious. Jesus. What a sight.

"Turn around. Hands behind your back."

She did exactly as he told her. Then he was behind her, his body pressed tight against hers, his hard-on pressing against her ass. He moved his foot between hers, and roughly kicked her legs apart. What she could only assume was his baton slid up her calves, then her inner thighs, and stopped just below her pussy, before he moved it up quickly, making her go up on her toes.

"You're an ass," Elena purred, not really meaning it.

Then there were hands on her wrists, the cold steel of the cuffs around one wrist, then the other, him pulling at her arms roughly, although she offered no resistance. The sounds of passing traffic and her idling car ceased to register with the click of the cuffs. Not fuzzy fun cuffs, not edible cuffs, no: police issue handcuffs. The real deal. Christ. Her clit was already twitching, her pussy already watering.

"Move!" he snarled, his breath hot on her ear.

He dragged her past her car to the other side of his. He pushed her forward so she was bent over the hood. His hand at the back of her neck grabbed a handle of hair. Shoving her head down, he pushed her cheek against the warm metal of the hood.

"Stay there," he barked, and stepped away.

She didn't move. She watched as he went to her car and turned off her lights, then did the same to his, but left the roof lights flashing. His radio crackled to life and a voice, barely audible, emitted from it. He talked into the radio on his shoulder. Jackson was all calm professionalism—not at all the same man who had her bent over the car.

"Just finishing a traffic violation. I'll be done in ten."

Then he was back behind her again, grabbing her by her hips and tugging at her pants until they were around her ankles. The cool fall air kissed her skin, goose bumps erupting on her flesh.

She heard him rip into what must be a condom wrapper, heard him fumbling with his belt and pants. She squeezed and clenched her pussy, convinced she could get off without him touching her.

"Stop that," he growled, and swatted her ass, hard, throwing the condom wrapper at her, which came to rest on the hood, inches from her cheek.

"Fuck," she grunted, under her breath.

Then his fingers grazed her pussy lips, already slick with her juices. He grabbed a handful of her hair, pulled her head back, and bit into her neck.

"I'm going to fuck you," he spoke in her ear, pushing her head back down so her cheek was again kissing the hood.

Then he was inside her, quick, hard, and unrelenting.

In a fleeting moment of logic, she wondered how this would appear if another car were to pull up behind them. Maybe it looked like she was being restrained. Who the hell cared anyway? She was bent over the hood of a squad car, getting fucked roughly by a policeman. This was the stuff fantasies were made of.

Now the traffic noises were drowned out by her whimpers, the rushing sound in her ears and the loud slapping of skin on skin.

"You're going to come hard, little girl," Jackson grunted, slowing down his thrusts, while again grabbing and tugging at her hair.

"Come on. Come for me." He thrust again, hard and fast.

And she came—came like she hadn't in a long time, a noise emitting from her that sounded like a mix of pleasure and pain, her legs shaking as her pussy clenched and tightened, clenched and tightened in sweet rolling waves.

He was unrelenting, fucking her even harder than before. He held tightly to her hips, his fingertips digging into her skin as he moaned through his orgasm; then he withdrew from her quickly, grabbed another handful of ass and spanked her lightly.

Again, she heard him fumbling with his clothes. He pulled up her panties and jeans, finally turning her to face him as he fastened her pants.

He kissed her hard and fast on the lips, then spun her around again, releasing her from the cuffs. Then he was walking away from her, all business again. Her blood was still pumping in her ears, her breath coming out in shallow grunts.

"Elena?" he said, turning to look at her again.

"Yeah?" she managed to sputter out.

"You still coming over at ten?"

"You really need to ask?"

"Guess not," he replied, smiling, impossibly cute. "I'll see ya later."

TEXTUAL INTERCOURSE

Magenta Brown

The year 2005 had been a slow one for me. I'd reached the age where, as an actress, I was no longer considered for romantic leads but was still too young to play anything else and consequently, I'd experienced a serious decline in work offers, not to mention auditions.

Several of my classmates from drama school were now in telesales and real estate, a few were teaching (acting classes mostly), and two particularly vivacious girls were allegedly doing double act porn in California.

Only, I wasn't ready for porn and I wasn't wanted for panto, which is how I found myself in the role of Text Sex Operator, sending saucy text messages to strangers for one pound fifty a pop.

Aside from my obsession with literacy—

sadly, most of my clients don't know a comma from their colon let alone know how to spell even the simplest words— text sex pays better than waitressing and is infinitely more dignified for a woman in her thirties.

I do wonder though, how does a clerk from a DIY store afford over twenty quid a day on messages? And come to think of it, why would someone using a fantasy wank service insist on keeping things so real? Why say you work at Homebase when you can pretend you're a city broker who wants to bend my slutty alter ego over his desk and bang me till I beg for mercy?

I don't want to know the truth about these people, and I'm sure as hell not sharing mine.

What I look like:

Hi babes, I'm 23 with light brown hair, green eyes & a really toned body! I have long, slim legs & am 5'8", 34d, love oral & outdoor sex!! Amy x
or
Hi babes, I'm 34. blonde, blue eyes & I'm really curvy. I love sexy lingerie, am 5'2", 36c, love sucking cock & shaven sex!! Lucy x

What I'm wearing:

Right now I'm dressed in my usual office gear, short skirt, knee-hi black leather boots & a little blouse with buttons up the front but they keep popping open!
or
I've just made it home from dance class & I'm wearing a thong, hot pants & a crop top—about 2 have a shower—

wanna join me?

What I'm doing:

Hi there sexy!! I'm chilling & watching hot porn with my flatmates, the girls are @ a bit of a loose end tonight. Wanna play?
or
Right now my hands are under my desk & inside my panties. I gotta get home but don't know whether 2 wank now or wait till i can really go 4 it? help me!

As you can tell, I'm not sticking to the truth. *(Hi I'm an out of work actress, u might know me from episodes of Holby City & The Bill, currently wearing pyjamas, supplementing my income during a particularly dry spell.)*
No way; as far as the punters know I'm a nurse (a very common fantasy), a bored housewife (equally popular), or a student who's also a stripper. On one service people actually think they're texting Jordan—I would have thought my unfailingly correct use of apostrophes (I can't help it) would have been a dead giveaway that I'm not Katie Price.
But it's not all bad news and sometimes I actually share texts with people who turn me on, people who make me reach down my knickers, wishing my fingers were somebody's tongue—incidentally, if you don't already know, this is done on a laptop, not a mobile, and sometimes I refer to myself as a lap(top) dancer.
And what makes this job particularly easy, now that I've been at it awhile: I've saved hundreds of responses so I make a point of leading punters into particular fantasies—a striptease, a little

light S/M, a secret screw in the office—then it's simply cut and paste all the way home.

Even as I write this I'm simultaneously firing little pearls of filth into the ether to over twelve different guys.

Interestingly, nearly everyone who texts eventually asks for a date, wants a phone number, or begs to meet, but up till now I've never felt tempted to arrange a rendezvous. It's sad how some guys fall for the make believe, but I don't feel bad about it; I mean, this is no more immoral than a cosmetic that promises to make people look younger—it's all lies, the world is built on bullshit.

To be fair though, it's not just sad, raincoat-wearing, friend-less, forty-year-old virgins who cross my path and every now and then I do actually find a client who turns me on. That's where this story really begins.

Recently, I received a text from a guy who was working late with a female colleague putting the finishing touches on a pro-posal and, to liven things up, we were sharing texts, mainly about what I'd do to him if I were to come down to the office.

I told this guy, Mark, how I'd get past security by masquer-ading as a pizza delivery girl and how, once inside, I'd tie him to a chair—resistance would be futile.

His female colleague, I warned him, would be much too stunned to stop me or even say anything.

And so the fantasy went on, him texting back describing her and his growing state of arousal, and me taking it further and further with each response.

Once he was tied up, I said, I'd tell her she could do anything she liked to him. Or if she preferred, she could tell me what to do to him and just watch. In our text fantasy, this was what she first chose. She made me cut all his clothes off with scissors;

he'd be scared but once the last stitch was snipped from his body we'd find him hard as a rock, gagging for attention.

This went on over a number of nights. In some variations I'd just strip for him, just to tease him, to be a bitch; and then I'd get it on with her, not letting him in on the action at all; or I'd thrust my perfectly trimmed bush into his face, one foot either side of his legs, forcing him to lick me to orgasm; or I'd suck him off or fuck him facing him, from behind, every which way under the sun. And what I learned was how much I loved the whole office domination thing—I was in charge and at the same time, at the mercy of these two as well.

And then I had an idea: I told him he had to show his colleague all the messages we'd shared—it was the moment of truth. He insisted he couldn't, but he was so used to being my slave it didn't take much to persuade him that he didn't have any choice.

Another text arrived and this time it was from her.

Hi this is Susie. I've read your texts, the ones you've been sending Mark, he told me he was being sent football results!

Well, Susie wasn't giving much away. I wasn't sure how to respond but with only 45 seconds and 175 characters with which to reply, I countered swiftly:

So what do you think Susie? U want a pizza this evening? x

For a moment I even forgot it was a fantasy and I was briefly concerned about what she might think or how she might respond. She probably didn't even exist!

She replied:

I love it, don't tell Mark I said this but he is so cocky, good looking but full of himself, I'd love 2 c him tied up. xxx

Her message included a financial district office address complete with suite number, and I answered without thinking:

Then I'd love 2 oblige. Shall we make a date 2 surprise him, play this game our way?

To this day I can't say why I did what I did next, why it seemed like such a good idea. I mean, text operators are always making dates with punters, to meet them outside this tube or on that bridge. I know it's cruel to let some poor schmuck stand around in the cold for a few hours, to get his hopes up only to dash them, but sometimes it's the only way you can get a guy to shut up about meeting, or get the message across that it's make believe without coming right out and saying, "Dude, don't be a halfwit."

Which is why I'll never know why I not only agreed to meet this couple, but immediately began to follow through.

First, I ordered a pizza to be sent to their office. Next, I texted a friend and told her exactly where I'd be. I texted Susie I'd done that, too, just in case she and Mark were planning anything weird.

Then I chose my outfit with care and precision: a simple black push-up bra, sheer black high-cut panties with suspenders and fishnets, a classic look. Over it all, a plain black, belted trench coat and a pair of heels so high I practically needed oxygen to wear them.

I didn't bother with perfume though: if there's one thing I can't stand it's licking, biting, kissing, and sucking someone's neck and getting a mouthful of aftershave or scent. Not sexy.

In my bag I packed some lengths of rope, a gag, and a few other surprises including dental dams, condoms, and lube. Then I called a cab.

As we drove through Central London, rather than wonder what the hell I was doing, I congratulated myself for having had a full wax just days before. I arrived at their building just in time to intercept the pizza man—perfect timing.

It wasn't too late to back out but I was so horny by this stage it was all I could do not to straddle the security guy and grind myself to orgasm on his lap. Instead, my trench coat tightly belted, I brandished the pizza and told him I was here on business and wasn't sure the call out was legit, so could he keep an eye out and, if he heard any screaming or whatever, sound the alarm?

In the lift, headed for the thirty-second floor, I had a chance to check that there was no lipstick on my teeth, that my eyelashes were holding and everything was where it should be.

The elevator sounded my arrival and opened onto an open-plan office, a vast space designed to be as creative as possible—meaning very little real work ever gets done.

And there they were: Mark and Susie in the flesh, and they sure weren't what I was expecting. He was thinning on top, whereas I'd envisaged a thick thatch of dark hair, and she was a bit older and slimmer than I'd imagined, but she had great breasts with a cleavage that was really something to behold. I can't have been what they were expecting either—I'm not blonde, twenty-three, or a nurse—and there I stood, holding a pizza box, wearing a trench coat and black stilettos and very little else.

The tension was so thick you could have cut it with a—pizza cutter; nobody said anything until eventually I broke the ice with a throaty hi.

They both said hi back.

"You order a pizza? With extras?"

Susie managed to speak first. "Yeah, that's right, you can put it on that desk."

I did.

She went to her purse and that's when I knew she was going to be fun. She turned back to me and, her acting better than any porn star I'd ever seen, said, "But we don't seem to have any money."

"How about a check?" I suggested.

"Sorry, no can do." Mark was in on it now.

"Well you're going to have to find some other way to pay me, aren't you?"

And once we all knew our parts it really started to flow.

"Perhaps we should discuss this inside." Susie led me to the corner office, and Mark followed, closing the door.

"What did you have in mind?" I asked, and Susie showed me exactly what she had in mind.

Slowly she unbuttoned her blouse, and her breasts were every bit as magnificent as I'd imagined when I first set eyes on her.

I let my trench coat fall open, and as I moved they both caught glimpses of just how provocatively I'd dressed for this. Mark started to unbutton himself too but Susie and I shared a wavelength and we shook our heads at him. I took the ropes from my bag and together Susie and I tied him to a chair—not too tight, but he wasn't going anywhere.

He started to say something, but I hate guys who rabbit on during sex so I took the gag, a length of silk, and shut him up with that.

He was cute but Susie was absolutely beautiful; I advanced on her slowly and kissed her once gently on the lips, so soft. We kissed like that for I don't know how long while my hands found their way to her thighs and slowly I raised her skirt, revealing first her legs and next her panties.

She pulled away, and I wondered if she was getting nervous,

but she just wanted to wriggle out of her skirt and blouse, to stand before me in just her underwear. I couldn't let a lady strip on her own, and I let my coat fall to the floor. Behind me I could hear Mark making some kind of noise but we ignored him. I sank to my knees and buried my face in Susie's bush, pulling her panties aside and inhaling the vanilla musk of her. I ran my fingers inside her slit, and she was so wet I wished for a moment I was a guy with a rock-hard cock.

Grabbing a dam, I went to work on her, licking and nibbling and sucking her sweet pussy through it till she was bucking into my face like she couldn't get enough. She was moaning like she was going to come sometime soon: the great thing about girls eating pussy, we know exactly what works and what doesn't.

Mark was really gurgling away about something now, so Susie generously took his index finger and started easing it in and out of her hot mouth, which helped send her over the edge as I furiously circled her clit with my tongue, four of my fingers inside her, feeling her cunt muscles squeezing me so tight. And as she came, so sweetly, Mark, to his undoubted chagrin, came too, just from our show and a little finger sucking. What a lightweight.

And then we heard the telltale ding of the elevator—it was the security guy. Susie and I wriggled back into our clothes faster than lightning and poor Mark just sat there, bound and gagged, a damp, dark patch spreading on his trousers like shame.

We've arranged to meet again. This time I think I'll be a cycle courier: "Can someone sign for this package?"

IN SNOW

Teresa Lamai

In December, Portland is washed in silver mist, cloistered in evergreens. Camellias are already blooming in every lawn, their pink scentless petals like shavings of soap, falling over the wet grass. Snails wander in slow patterns over the sidewalks at night. I step over them carefully. On hushed dark mornings like this, they don't quite realize it's daytime yet.

The downtown streets are empty, silent except for the distant hissing of the trolley. The mist seems to swallow every sound. The Christmas lights over the theater are dark. Jim, the night security guard, is still on duty, ignoring the monitors and deep into his crossword puzzle. I've brought him a coffee and I pass it through the half-open Plexiglas window at his booth. I can't stop to chat but he raises a donut in greeting before I run down the dusty hallway, my breath and footsteps echoing harshly.

I'm the first one in the dressing room. When I flick on the lights, the room buzzes faintly. We have two performances today, matinee and evening shows of the *Nutcracker*. The room seems stunned into silence, as if still recovering from the mass of terror, pain, and elation that filled it last night. I need this quiet time to breathe and let my mind narrow down into the tiny, essential rituals of preparation: makeup, hair, tape. I take out my makeup kit first. The false eyelashes are sleeping prettily in their pink box.

I pause and reach into my purse. Folded in between receipts is Christian's note, the one he left on my bedside table three days ago. I haven't read it yet. I press it against my forehead. Memory wells up from my body and surfaces in my mind, brightly.

The rustle of paper was what woke me that morning, the last time I was with him. I rolled toward him as he sat carefully on the bed's edge. He was already dressed, already wrapped in his gray wool coat, his white hair brushed, his starched collar chaffing his freshly shaven neck. There was a sideways freezing rain outside; wet branches lashed against the window. His profile in the predawn gloom was like a sepia-washed portrait. I caught his hand and he turned quickly, his eyes shadowed and glittering. I pulled at the tight leather glove until it finally gave way. His thick pale fingers tasted like soap. When they touched the back of my throat my sleepy cunt pulsed twice.

When I reached for his zipper, his cock was already lengthened, arched taut like a bow, straining against the cloth. I unzipped, watching it uncurl and slide against his black silk shorts. I freed it into my mouth, licking up the shaft. I inhaled, deeply. Squeaky clean. When my lazy hand closed around the base, I felt the blood pumping steadily. The zipper bit at me. I lifted myself, resting my head on his lap, pressing my breasts into his thigh. The heavy duvet fell away. As his skin warmed, it gave off the scent of shampoo, then his own rich smell, savory and spicy, the hint of anise and warm vanilla.

His hand spread over my tousled head. The other, still gloved, reached under the duvet and quickly found my sex. It was slick from the night before, the clit still sore and restless. Two fingers slid into my wet cunt. The leather was smooth as oil. His thumb brushed the damp hair over my mound, tickling, letting the clit swell tight before he covered it in slow, meticulous circles. I rocked against him, my moans quiet around his cock.

When he tugged on the tendrils over my neck, I came, startling myself. I arched back, helpless, loud, letting his cock bounce out of my mouth. I covered him with my mouth again, breathing hard, letting my tongue slip over the satiny head. He smoothed my hair with his heavy warm palm, murmuring softly down to me.

He wrapped my hair in his fist as he came. I swallowed everything.

My eyes were closed but I felt his body lift off the bed. I rolled onto my back. My lips were salty. I didn't want to open my eyes and see him go. He fit his palms over my cheekbones. I turned my head to suck on the wet leather.

His mouth was on mine. I hadn't realized I was crying until I felt the tears sliding over my temples.

I swallowed. "Hurry back."

"You know I will." His hand squeezed over my throat

once, slid down to my stomach, and he was gone.

It feels like he's been gone for months. His conference will be over in early January, just after New Year's. At first I was relieved we'd be apart during the holidays; as new lovers, for us the questions of families and gifts would have been fraught with awkwardness. Now I have to admit to myself that I feel a bit lost without him.

I hear a noise in the hallway and I'm back in the present, blinking at myself in the mirror. Someone's opening the dressing room door. I tuck Christian's note away and sit upright, clearing my throat, fussing with my makeup kit.

Trinh bursts in, panting. Her dance bag is wider than she is.

"Hi, baby-doll." She hugs me from behind, leaning her cheek against mine. Her young face is still shining with mist. She squints in the makeup mirror's lights.

I squeeze her hand before she lets go. She's trying not to look nervous. Which makes her look more nervous. This is her first year with a solo, Drosselmeyer's doll.

"I'm going to totally suck in the solo today. Just so you know." Trinh will leave for a performing arts college this spring. This is our last performance together. Our first was the year I joined the company; she was cast as an angel along with the other intermediate girls.

"Totally suck," she repeats gaily, dragging a chair up next to mine, tucking her bag under the counter.

"Ah, no," I answer, on cue. I'm lining my eyes but I watch her in the mirror, my head tilted and motionless. "Rather you will, in fact, rock like a big rock-star-resembling ballerina."

She hugs me again, squeezing my shoulders. Her eyes are narrow and wet. The pressure makes me exhale sharply.

"Okay, ow."

"You're just saying that 'cause you love me."

"That too."

I open my powder box, smiling carefully. I realize I'm still in the habit of keeping my face pleasant and peaceful around the other dancers in the company. The ghost of my marriage has troubled this haphazard family deeply, and for longer than I had ever expected. Mark and I had been the only married couple in the ballet company, at least ten years older than most of the dancers in the corps. We never fought. Mark especially was adored by the kids. The cheekiest of the little ones would call us ma and pa.

It's been over two years since Mark and I officially divorced. As his technique slipped, as his dreams of national-level success faded, he found comfort in chemically manufactured happiness. He started with prescriptions but street supplements were more powerful, and cheaper. At first, everyone else still saw the sunny, winsome Mark, but at home it was becoming a nightmare—absurd and terrifying and never-ending. Alcohol I could justify to myself, maybe pot, but heroin made him into a monster with raw, colorless eyes. Meth made him scream at things that weren't there.

I didn't know how to tell anyone. Soon I didn't have to. The night Mark was arrested for DUI, I packed him an overnight bag, posted his bail, and dropped him off at his brother's. I told him to stop using or leave. I couldn't quite believe it was me saying the words. That was the last time I saw him.

I slept long and often in the quiet cottage after he left. Everyone tried to assure me that, at thirty, I still had so much to look forward to, but somehow the future ceased to be a part of my thinking. My life just narrowed down to a series of discrete moments, like mismatched beads on a thread: class, coffee, sunset, phone call. I stopped looking for any pattern, any meaning that would unite it all and give it momentum.

A few more sleepy dancers are wandering into the dressing room. I'm almost finished putting on my makeup. Dark brown shadow, silver highlights just under the brows. The tiara is lopsided again, and I try to straighten its tiny plastic wires, holding it up and squinting. It's supposed to suggest the crystals of a snowflake, yet be regal enough to indicate that I am in fact the Snow Queen. Instead it's looking like a souvenir from a bachelorette party.

I'm humming to myself. I love the snow scene.

Mark and I used to dance the Snow pas every year. Paul, our company's director, was in a panic when Mark left. There was suddenly no Snow King, three weeks to opening night. He tried to reassure me but I heard him in his office, his genial, effete voice growing strained, as he telephoned all his old contacts. Good male dancers are hard to come by in this season.

"I can rework it into a solo," I said, and showed him.

Paul stood up when I was finished and gripped my shoulders. He kissed my wet forehead as I panted. "Oh, thank god, Kathryn, I knew I could count on you."

It's been a solo ever since, I suspect because it's cheaper that way. I've come to enjoy it more than any other show; being onstage alone is like opening a swift, lightning-hot current of excitement. There's a feeling of control, mastery—and possibility; I could very well ditch the choreography and do whatever the fuck I'm moved to do. It's spurred me to finally start working on my own pieces.

Last year, when I finished the winter season, Portland was having one of its weird, early springs. I noticed the new bookstore, just at the end of my street. Cherry blossoms and holly branches crowded the entrance, hanging rich and low. The inside was full of dry heat, scented with tea and caramel. Books—new, secondhand, and antique—were stacked to the ceiling, heaped like a miser's gold. I stopped in nearly every evening on my way home.

Christian, I guessed, was the owner. It was his stillness that I noticed first, a serene, focused energy that made him seem the center of any space. People gathered around him unconsciously, bright eyed. He was tall and slender, with a voice so deep and soft you felt it more than you heard it, an almost subsonic resonance that always distracted me and made me want to stop moving and listen. His hair was light blond, streaked with white, waving to thick autumn gold curls at his neck. When he smiled, his russet brown eyes sparkled like burgundy. I started looking forward to his smiles.

I didn't admit to myself, at first, that I was dressing carefully before going in, that I really didn't need so many books. I eavesdropped as he chatted with customers, closing my eyes and imagining myself alone with that voice, that smile, somewhere shadowed and secluded.

I kept telling myself I would stop visiting the store, stop plaguing this poor stranger with my melancholy, eager self. I kept stopping by. Piles of books started spilling over onto my couch and my carpets.

One evening, I felt him standing behind me. My back warmed as if a swath of sunlight had fallen on it. I had a crazy urge to lean into his chest. My palms were tingling.

"I've been trying to find some kind of pattern in the books you choose, but I can't." He sounded amused, but his voice dropped low, as if he were sharing an urgent secret.

"Oh, I just take whatever seems to jump out at me. I don't

want to be systematic." I was proud of myself for sounding so casual. I even turned and glanced at his shirt buttons, then up to his face. "It's more fun when you let things surprise you."

"That's true." His voice was softer, and careful. I tried very hard not to stare at his mouth. "But then sometimes something will really speak to you, and you have to find the courage to follow it."

I turned back toward the shelves. My heart sank. I put back my book while I waited for him to continue, to segue into the patronizing editorial that I would interrupt with the closing door. It was really time for dinner anyway.

He was silent. I turned around. His mouth was a tight, solid line, but his eyes were bright. His pale golden freckles gleamed.

"But you know that, of course." His smile spread from his eyes. He was radiant.

"I'm going to be taking all these." I gathered up an armload of paperbacks, without breaking his gaze.

"Wait for me to close and I'll help you carry them home."

The memory recedes and I bite my lip. It might be a bad idea to let myself remember Christian so vividly here in the dressing room. My cunt is waking up, swelling fitfully against my fresh pink tights. My nipples are tightening. I'm stroking powder over my forehead, my eyes going dull.

Trinh has been singing low for a few moments now, watching me in the mirror. The dressing room is filling with anxious bodies and the scents of peppermint oil and deodorant. My hair is finished, the last wisps plastered down. I shake my head quickly and add a few more bobby pins. I put in rhinestone earrings.

"*Working at the car wash,*" Trinh sings, wrapping her

toenails. She looks at me again, knowing I'll laugh soon.

"Work, and work," she's singing more loudly. "Come on, Kathy. Do the car wash with me."

"Oh, for god's sake."

She jumps out of her chair, swiveling her hips so that her tutu swishes loudly. *"The boss don't mind if you play the fool,"* she sings. I roll my eyes. Laughter wells up around us.

"Yeah, not right now." I'm the perfect straight man for her shtick. I grab my coffee. "I have to go. Old people have to actually warm up."

"Do my bun later?" Trinh calls after me. There are a few echoes of "Mine too?"

"Okay." I pad up the metal stairwell. I'm wearing thick wool over my legs, oversized socks over my pointe shoes, an old flannel shirt. The older dancers, the principals, are already out on the cool, empty stage, lying on their stomachs or in splits, rubbing their hips with Ben-Gay. Their children play school in the empty seats.

I smile but I don't join the conversation. I pretend to need the solitary barre in the wings but in fact I just want to relive memories of Christian on my own. I feel like a greedy little girl sneaking the last slice of cake into her room to eat in private. I lift my leg on the barre and lean my forehead into the scratchy leg warmer, closing my eyes.

We kissed that first evening, standing just inside my door, clinging together. His kisses were deliciously thorough. I slid my belly against his until I felt his cock pressing against my pubic bone. I giggled with my own daring, skittish and out of breath. He held my temples and rested his forehead on mine, whispering goodnight.

I went to bed quickly. Making love then would have been

too much. Instead I held his memory and scent close, reaching into my hungry sex until I came very quietly.

Six weeks later we still had done nothing more than kiss. I didn't know how to tell him I wanted him; it seemed too obvious for words. I began to suspect he was playing a game, waiting for me to make a fool of myself. My stomach was cold with uncertainty but my cunt was always restless, neglected, and seething.

One night, as I kissed his warm fragrant neck, drawing my tongue over the wiry stubble, I caught his wrist and fit my breast into his palm. He pulled back, inhaling. My frustration flared. I stood clumsily, then looked down at him.

"Maybe you'd better go, Christian."

I turned off the video player and the wind moaned, shoving and rattling at the windows. The firelight pushed faintly at the heavy blue shadows, guttering in the draft.

He was a black shape, unmoving. I sat again, just at the edge of the couch, uncertain.

His breathing slowed.

"Kathy, will I ever know you?"

I was silent. What kind of game was this?

His hands moved over my shoulders, closing tight. I reached for him, but he pressed me back into the sofa, sitting up and turning toward me. His cheek and temple glowed amber in the firelight. The more quietly he spoke, the more I felt it like a low current in my skin.

"I don't want to just be pleased and then sent away."

I was pissed off now. I looked at the ceiling, watching the crisscrossed shadows wave. *I assume there's a point you're trying to make*, I thought. But I didn't trust my voice not to shake.

"I want more than that, Kathy. And I know you do, too. I want to feel all of you, even the parts that scare you. Kathy, believe me, I want everything you have to give, everything you are."

I sat upright, looking away, holding my palm rigidly toward him—a wordless, shaking imperative. I let it settle on his chest, unsure whether I was resting on him or keeping him away.

He let one hand fall through my hair and rest, gently, against my throat.

"I want to know where you would go if you weren't afraid. What you think about in private when raw, selfish lust finally wins out."

His voice dropped. I felt his breath on my cheek. My feet twitched.

"I want to know what knocks you sideways, what makes your cunt wet." My mouth opened. Heat filled my chest, tight and heavy. My sex pulsed as if his lips were on it.

His fist closed in my hair, just at the crown of my head. He pulled gently at the scalp until tears came to my eyes, and let his fingertips sink deeper into my neck. Desire made the flaring ceiling go dim. I could smell my own wetness as it bled through my panties.

When he leaned back, I saw his eyes.

"Stay here, Christian. I want you to stay here."

"Do you want to stand up and get undressed, Kathy?" A rush of icy sweetness followed his voice down my spine. My nipples burnt like coals.

I swallowed against his hard palm. "Yeah."

I did, quickly, before my mind could catch up to my body. The fire was warm on my back. He asked for my stockings.

He caressed my wrists.

"Kathy—"

"Yes, yes."

I squeezed my eyes shut as he stood and tied my wrists together, stretching the nylon tight. I heard him get up on the coffee table to bring the ends over the ceiling beam, pulling away the ivy and pothos vines. As he stepped down, I turned and leaned my forehead into my cool upper arm. My legs shuddered. I bit the inside of my cheek and willed my heart to beat more quietly. Any thoughts I tried to form were torn and sucked away swiftly, like dead leaves in the first winter storm.

I didn't know where he was. My skin contracted and tingled over my stomach, my thighs. I wondered where I would feel his touch first.

"Kathy, look at me. It's all right." He was in front of me. He brushed the hair from my face.

"Look up," he said. The nylon was twisted over the rough wood, knotted and filled with splinters. My hands were pink and half-curled.

"Pull. Try to pull your hands away." He moved behind me. My hair cooled as he blocked the fire's heat. Sweat was pooling at the base of my spine.

"I want you to pull, Kathy." He stepped back. A streak of pain blazed across my ass. I think I cried out. I struggled to breathe in. He must have put the full weight of his back into the blow. I was pulling instinctively now, desperate to cover myself. My wrists were raw. My throat was cold and ragged as if I had swallowed sharp ice. My cunt was on fire.

"That's right, beautiful Kathy, hold on, hold on, and pull." He laid his palms flat over my ass. The pain turned to stinging warmth that washed down my legs, making them weak. As he moved in front of me again, he trailed three fingers over my hip. My labia squeezed painfully between my tight, slippery thighs. I couldn't stop panting. The dim room was going black.

"Hold on, it's all right. It will be all right, Kathy, I promise." He sank to his knees.

I came twice with just his fingers. Heat seared through me so violently that I started to panic. When the stars started sparking and flying in front of my eyes I gripped the nylon to keep from falling. I looked down at him as he lifted my thigh and rested it over his rumpled, heated shoulder.

"Don't make me come again." The small, slurred voice slipped out of me before I could control it. "Don't. Don't. I can't take it."

He turned and kissed the inside of my thigh, as it tensed over his shoulder. He murmured so low I could barely hear him. His touch became almost chaste, soothing; he ran his palms over my lower back and let his lips fall softly over my thigh.

When my breathing quieted, he rested his cheek on my leg and looked up at me with strangely serene eyes. His smooth fingers followed the swell of my ass and tickled into the slick cleft, delicate as kitten paws. My stomach rippled.

"Shh, Kathy, shh. It's all right." His breath played over the black glossy curls but he kept his eyes on mine.

When he dragged his tongue between the fat, burning labia, squeezing the clit between two patient fingers, I came again, shrieking, pulling the beam so hard it creaked.

He stood, resting his hands on my hips. His chin was shining and his eyes were dilated.

I thought he would fuck me then but he reached for my
wrists, finally pulling them free. I fell forward and clutched at
his shirt until the placket tore and it slid from his wide shoulders. My knees gave way and I knelt, shaking, working the
thick wool off his legs.

Christian, naked, was golden all over. His skin was the
color of heavy cream, smooth and gleaming along the supple length of his back. The twin swells of his cool ass caught
the light like white gold. Over his chest and belly, auburn and
white hair curled, thick gilt fur. It glittered with his sweat, dif-
fusing the firelight around him like a halo.

His balls trembled in my palm like a captured bird. His
cock slid into my impatient mouth, smooth as sun-warmed
marble and clinging soft as velvet.

When his balls tightened under my fingers, he gently pulled
my head away. My mouth was still open as I fell back on the
carpet. I pulled on his hips until he tumbled after me, breaking his fall with his hands. I locked my ankles behind him, digging my heels into his back as I lifted my hips. My cunt drew
him in, clenching; my hands couldn't get enough of his skin. I
cried when he finally dipped his head down, resting his sweat-
drenched forehead on my breastbone, pushing into me until
my heart ached.

Every time I remember that night, I find myself dragging my
fingernails down the back of my neck, just enough to hurt. I
let my nails sink into the tender flesh under the hairline. When
I hear myself suck in my breath with an urgent hiss, I jump a
little. The memory recedes quickly. I hear voices; utility lights
are warming the stage.

Warm-up class is already starting. I'm standing here, hog-
ging a barre, leaning my cheek on my wool-covered thigh. I

carry the barre over toward the others as we set up for the first exercises. I hope I'm not blushing too obviously.

I think again of Christian's wadded note, now probably lying at the bottom of my dance bag. I still haven't read it. It's not like him to write something for me.

I try to shake the dread and promise that keep crowding my thoughts of him lately. Together, we seem to create a perfect circle of understanding, passion, and discovery. But I can't help the way my imagination keeps running ahead of itself, as if trying to find ways we can give each other even more. I think it's the season, all the gifts and celebrations—the relentless hinting that there will always be something hidden in the frozen dark.

Thankfully, class is starting and I'm distracted.

When I return to the dressing room, it's packed. A thick steam of hairspray and nervous sweat hangs just under the ceiling. Jeff, our newest dancer, has wandered in and he's reclining on the love seat, his thick legs splayed out. The girls are arranged around him, already in costume, like a nest of rippling, giggling, candy-hued tulle. Even those who pretend to ignore him have shifted closer.

"I've taught myself a song," he says, hefting a guitar into his lap. He's wearing a faded hoodie over his costume. He loves the eyeliner; he looks more like an eighties rock star than a ballet dancer.

He strums, nodding gravely. He makes a valiant attempt to sing along but his hands can't keep pace with the rhythm in his mind. Most chords take three or four tries.

"*I wanna fuck you like an an*—wait—*an*—wait—*ani*—wait—*muuuuuhhhl.*"

The others scream with laughter. Crystal, an apprentice,

glances in my direction and bites her lip. She thinks that, as an old lady, I'll be offended by the fuck word.

I sit with my back to them, furtive and skittish, and reach into my bag. I won't read it now. Yes, I will. A small breath of silence settles over my shoulders as I unfold it.

Kathy, I need to tell you that the love I have for you is transforming me. I want to try and make you understand this, and it feels as though it would take a very long time to do so properly. Please let me.

I read it three times before it even starts to reach my mind. I press my hands over my face. His wording is so labored and so utterly sincere at the same time, so much like him it makes me want to hug myself.

The overture music is starting, piped down from the house on a tiny, cracked speaker. Everyone is motionless for two quick beats. This moment always brings a rush of terror, like the hot wind before a forest fire. I hate to stew in all that panic. Before the chaos can ramp up again, I slip upstairs to watch from the wings.

The shadows offstage are chilly, but nervous tension warms me. I take off my flannel shirt. I strip off the rest of the wool and jump in place, swinging my arms. The harp arpeggio starts; eight more bars. I check my tights. I clench my fists and shake them out, lifting my abs up toward my ribs.

This is when the wave of panic hits. I usually fight it down, like nausea, but tonight I let it rise, crest, and then spread through me. When it washes away, there is nothing but stillness. The light changes, that's my cue.

It's one of those nights when the stage is warm as a mineral bath. Time distends strangely; the variation seems to last for hours. I'm startled when it's over, as if I expected to end up somewhere other than the center of the first panel, under the blue spotlight, with fake plastic snow sticking to my false lashes.

The snow scene finishes Act I, and we're expected to come out into the lobby and have portraits taken with the children. I smooth on another layer of powder and run up the steel staircase.

The crowd is a mass of red and green velvet, shimmering gold jewelry, brisk new perfumes and steam from the espresso bar.

I can tell by the way my neck tingles that Christian is here. He doesn't seem surprised when I turn to him.

I lean my cheek on the front of his sweater. His chest lifts. He rests his hand on my tacky head.

"You're back early."

"I am." His voice is so quiet when he's happy.

The costume mistress is frantically gesturing me over to the photo set. I have to leave. I sit on the fiberglass chair and a series of toddlers scramble into my lap, one after another. They stare at the fake jewels on my tutu, grin wildly at the camera, show me their arabesques, and tell me as much about their lives as they can before their mothers pull them away. Their dusty little boots make tracks on my tights; I'll have to change when I'm done.

I've lost sight of Christian in the crowd, but it seems I can tell where he is by the soft, constant pull at my heart.

VICARIOUS

Lee Skinner

Pete, my *chef d'equipe,* is cheating on his wife with a woman he met on Amtrak. It started innocently—they shared a cab home one night in February after a storm shut down the train midway, at Roseville. The evening after that, the woman—Natalie—took the seat beside him, feeling obligated, Pete figured at the time, because he'd insisted on paying the whole fare. The third evening, they got off at a stop just outside the city and shared a hotel room for a couple of hours. Easy as that.

Easy for Pete, that is; impossible—unfathomable—for me. I like to tell myself it's because of my post; that a governor simply cannot do such things; that a life in the public eye precludes even the contemplation of anything requiring that degree of moral flexibility.

But the truth is, I simply don't know *how* to go from hello to horizontal with a woman in less than, say, five actual dates. I haven't got that kind of game. Never have had, never will have.

I told Pete as much, over Chinese takeout in his office.

He frowned at me, fork in the air, uncomprehending. "Whaddaya mean? We're not talking about finding your soul mate, here. We're talking about sex."

I smiled, wryly. "Not been there, ain't done that."

"Ain't done what?"

"Casual sex."

"Oh, come on." Pete rolled his eyes, then looked closer into mine, and saw that I was telling the truth. He whistled sympathetically, shaking his head.

When Pete met Natalie, he's quick to claim, sex was all that was on the agenda. He's married, she's married; the fact that sex was all either wanted was what had initially made the relationship so safe, and so honest. Until that same honesty—which neither of them had ever found with anyone else in their lives—gave the thing staying power, and made it complicated. Now Pete talked about her a lot.

I was the only person who knew, the only person he trusted. That exclusive honor meant Natalie came up in almost every private conversation we had.

I could see that he couldn't help it. Natalie-of-the-Amtrak, once a simple balm for the stress of Pete's job—which I'll freely admit is often more challenging than mine—had become someone who mattered. One lunch hour, when we'd had extra time and we'd scored the quiet table at Babur (the one where I can sit with my back to a bank of palms, and go the whole meal without shaking a single hand) he tried to explain it.

"It's being *wanted* again." He put his fork down, leaned against his side of the table. "Not that Pam doesn't want—I mean, things at home are good; I'm lucky, but...with Natalie..."

I waited, patient, for him to find the words. When you talk for a living like I do, you learn to love to listen. "Yes?"

"I thought I'd never be wanted in that way again. Loved, sure. But *desired*..."

He lowered his voice and leaned forward, and he looked younger, more vital somehow, than I'd seen him in the seven years we'd worked together.

"It's just *good*, Hal. Good for the soul. I feel like I've stolen a second helping of something I finished my fair share of long ago."

His words stayed with me all afternoon. On my drive home that night, he called me on my cell about a question he'd forgotten to ask. I was alone in the car, driving, the only time of my day that affords me any privacy. My wife, Katy, who thinks I need the rest, has been hounding me to hire a chauffeur. I won't. I need these forty minutes twice a day, with no one watching, no one waiting.

Pete waited on the other end of the line. "Hal? You there?"

"Huh? Mm-hmm. I was thinking about your girl."

"Nat?"

"Yeah." I smiled. "I think you've got to cut me off. I'm starting to feel like a voyeur."

He laughed. "It's my fault. I shouldn't be so free..."

"No. Not at all. We're friends. What would I do if I couldn't live vicariously through you?"

"I dunno. Cruise the Amtrak?"

I smiled wanly. "No can do."

"I know, guv'nor."

The next week the storm hit, and we were hip deep in disaster relief claims. We were on the road sixteen hours a day, visiting the communities that had suffered the worst of the flooding. It was an exhausting time, trying to be visible to our constituents, but at the same time needing to do the real work of negotiating the relief settlement with the feds.

I didn't envy Pete then. When I'd finally put my phone away, often after midnight, I imagined him in his own hotel room, still talking. I knew he was exhausted, weary with the weight of other people's misfortune. But he still had two lonely women to call; women he'd neglected for weeks now, who needed reassurance of his love.

No. That's not for me. I don't have the room in my life. I'm still young, I have a long way to go yet in this business. I can't afford to break any hearts. I'll make enough strategic mistakes as it is, without leaving behind disgruntled mistresses for my opponents to flush out.

And I won't risk hurting Katy. I need her support. I married a woman with the brains to back me up, and the independence to wait for me when I can't be there. I can't do anything to undermine her loyalty.

Don't get me wrong. I'm not coming from a high moral place. I'm a man like any other. Some days, I swear, I could fuck every woman I see. I could enjoy each and every one. If I were Pete, I'd be squeezing every last drop of pleasure out of what he has, this second chance of his. But *I* closed that door the day I threw my hat into the ring.

The greatest thing about the idea—the one that had Pete

squirming in the limo seat across from me, two weeks after the flood crisis—was that it came not from him, but from her. Natalie.

Sweat was literally beading on his brow. He cleared his throat. I waited for him to continue.

"And?"

"And..." he wiped his palms on his pants. "Hal, you've known me for seven years. You know I don't talk. What you say to me doesn't go any further."

I nodded. Of course I knew it.

"But she knows that you know about her. And the other day I was saying...well...that I don't envy you your careful life. That you can't have someone like her."

"And she said?"

He looked me in the eye. "She said maybe you can."

The plan was that we—the three of us—would have supper. Pete and I were on the road again, in a large town in the northwest part of the state. We would dismiss the staff, order in, and eat in his suite. Natalie would drive up and join us.

If I didn't like her, that would be it. She'd have supper with her lover and the governor; a pleasant evening, a night to remember. But if I *did*...

My hands shook a little as I loosened my tie. I slid it off in front of the mirror, watched the gray silk slip through my hands like a dropped lifeline. The comfort of my persona. The convenient excuse for a life of restraint. I dropped my cuff links into a clean ashtray; I rolled my sleeves. I looked for Pete's room key, but my eyes stopped on the minibar. I poured myself a double scotch; no ice to stand in its way when I knocked it back. Harsh—but I hoped it would ease the knot that was my stomach. I rapped firmly on the door to Pete's room.

She opened the door herself.

I grasped her hand, looked into her face. I've trained myself to be a quick study, to apply a name to a face so that it sticks. You wouldn't believe the power, in this business, of simply remembering someone. They'll all remember YOU; you're the governor. But if you can return the compliment—if you can pull the right name out of the mental file the next time you see the face—then bingo. She's on your team. Or getting there.

Natalie had olive skin, which caught me by surprise, although it shouldn't have. I knew her mother was from Sri Lanka, her father from Baton Rouge. She had long dark hair. One lock of it kept falling across her face as she ate, uncurling its way from behind her ear and tumbling across her cheek as she bent forward over her plate. She had good table manners. She ate slowly, waited until she was done chewing to answer a question. But there was nothing stiff about her. One time, when she thought I wasn't looking (I'm *always* looking) she speared an endive and touched it to Pete's lips, just for the pleasure of hearing the crunch of the delicate leaf between her lover's teeth. She smiled at him and I felt my own lips part, hungry. *Oh yes,* I thought. *I like you. Yes.*

I found myself staring at them, trying to read even one sign of the nerves that I myself felt, that I'd spent years of my life training myself to hide. But Pete was at ease; he was himself. He was no different around her than he was with me. He was my go-to guy, my trusted friend. And when Natalie spoke, her voice was steady and rich. When the conversation required it, she let her brown eyes meet mine.

We never talked about it. Not one word. The deal was

done in a single glance: a question in her eyes, a formality. I could see that she knew the answer but I gave it anyway, for the honor of accepting her extraordinary offer. *Yes I will, my lovely girl. And thank you.*

She smiled back, stood, and called room service to clear our meal. I busied myself with some snifters and brandy, my back to them on purpose. I knew her mind but I wasn't positive of his. I thought I'd give them a moment to deliberate.

Pete sat at the edge of the bed to tune the radio. I heard her move across the room, heard the bed creak as she lowered herself to his lap, heard him moan softly as her lips left his. They were less than six feet away.

I realized I was holding my breath and forced myself to exhale, inhale, exhale. The porter came in and took an eternity loading his cart. I was hard, obvious in my thin wool trousers; so I stood awkwardly, trying to casually keep my back to him and them at the same time. I was grateful for the excuse to go and put the chain on the door when he left; except it meant I had to walk directly back toward them.

When I turned, her eyes were on mine. We took three steps each, in synchronicity. I felt like I was on a treadmill, drawn forward by a commitment already made, a line already crossed. Natalie put her fingertips on my shoulders, stood on her toes like a dancer, and kissed me lightly on the mouth. And then she waited.

I looked past her, to Pete. He stepped forward in answer, and his hands moved to the zip at the back of Natalie's skirt. He pulled it down and she leaned back into his arms, letting the skirt drop to the floor as he kissed her ear, then lifted her hair to kiss the back of her neck.

She had stockings on, with stays and a garter belt. Worn for me, I knew. My taste, not Pete's. I knelt and lifted the edge of her blouse, looked for the ties at the sides of her panties that I knew would be there. In the morning, when I come to my office, the day's paperwork is organized just so, with the things I like to deal with first on top. Pete's handiwork. And here too, under Natalie's skirt: two little bows to untie so that the panties come off and the rest—stockings, belt, heels—stay on. A tiny detail from a rambling fantasy, disclosed once, years ago, the hour late, the bottle empty. This is why, if I have my way, Pete will always work with me.

I left the bows intact a moment. I hadn't even touched this woman yet. I put a hand on each ankle, trailed my fingers upward. She stood perfectly still, smiling. Her arms were over her head, entwined with his. His chin was buried in her hair.

Her panties were silk, bubblegum pink, eye level to me as I knelt. As my fingers left the thin mesh of her stockings for the warmth of her thighs, I watched a shadow begin to bloom there, a little heart-shaped watermark, a shade or two darker pink. I pressed my nose to it. She smelled of sleep, like a rumpled bed, pulling me in. I pulled the ties and the slip of fabric dropped away. I opened her with my tongue. She gasped. I felt Pete's eyes on me.

I licked her once more, my tongue wide and flat, and she crumpled to her knees, giggling. "Oh...! I can't. Not standing up. I'm sorry..."

We knelt together in a heap between the two beds, laughing, her hair half over her face. Pete sat on the bed behind her. She guided me to my feet, pulled the tails of my shirt free, worked the buttons expertly, then pulled her own blouse over her head. Her breasts were small; plum-colored nipples visible through the black lace of her bra. She had both of her small, cool hands around my cock. Pete watched.

Natalie guided me with her hands, sliding me further back on the bed. I reached up, unhooked her bra, the fabric catching for a second as I swept it across her nipples. She took my chin in one hand, turned my head so I could see myself in the headboard mirror. Then she knelt between my legs.

I watched her work; long strokes first, her tongue trailing all the way down to the crease of my thigh. I'd never watched someone blow me before. Her tongue swept lightly across the skin below my testicles and I had to force my legs still, my thighs flat, so they wouldn't block the view.

Pete was watching too, his hand on his belt now, his pants sliding to the floor. But by then I was deep in her mouth, and the effort to keep my eyes open was too much. I closed them, let my knees draw up, let my pelvis rise to meet her lips halfway on each stroke.

And then Natalie gasped, breaking the seal for a second, and I looked down to see Pete behind her, a hand on each of her hips, pulling her backward. Her lips slipped, a tight rosebud sliding down around my own glistening cock as he pulled her onto his. I grabbed handfuls of her hair, animal-like, unwilling to give her up. Her eyes widened, but she didn't let me go. Pete's next thrust eased her forward and I came suddenly and hard, hollering, eyes open, seeing nothing. He pulled her back again and I slid on the satin bedspread, landing on the floor between the beds.

Pete's a big, strong man. In one smooth motion he lifted and turned her, forced her onto him where he sat. Her hair covered his face like a curtain. They were oblivious to my presence. He held her narrow hips in each of his big hands, forcing her down as he thrust. They were inches away; I could see his cock disappear inside her and I willed myself hard again. I wanted to take her back for myself, but it was too soon.

And then it was over. She struggled for a second under his rough grasp, her legs painfully wide, escaping just before he came, spurting all over both of them and me. She laughed at the mess, the feminine timbre of her voice shocking in the testosterone-charged room. She lay back and looked into his eyes, ignoring me. She ran her fingers through his hair. He kissed her tenderly, circled one nipple with the tip of his tongue. But when he spoke, it was to me. "Hal?"

"Yes?"

He traced a finger across Natalie's thigh, leaving a glistening trail. "You wanna come help me clean up?"

Yes, I thought. *Yes I do. Thank you.*

PAID FOR THE PLEASURE

Adrie Santos

I couldn't believe I was doing it—responding to an ad at all, never mind such a strange one. I listened to his introduction one last time: "I am looking for serious replies only..." His voice was monotone—almost cold. "I am a fifty-two-year-old, average-looking man with a fetish for giving oral pleasure. I am seeking women who will allow me to come into their homes or a hotel to pleasure them orally and I expect nothing in return. I am also willing to compensate." That was it. It wasn't a particularly dynamic pitch, and not even remotely sexy by normal standards, yet I was drawn to it.

I had started using this telephone dating service one drunken night with some friends as a joke, and would on the occasional late night get on to kill some time and sometimes reply to ads with a message at best. Never had I dared to chat live.

My heart raced as I pressed *one* to request a live connection. I was nervous and incredibly excited at the thought of what I was about to get myself into. Being an attractive girl with everything most people would want—a great job and a beautiful place—might lead one to wonder why I would respond to such an ad, but I was wet at the mere idea, and determined to follow through.

"Thank you for getting back to me," he began. "Let me tell you about myself; I am fifty-two with an average build. My hair is gray and thinning. I wear glasses and consider myself to be very average looking. I am a business professional who has a fetish for giving oral pleasure. I am looking to meet ladies who will allow me to come over and eat them out with no strings attached. I have done this before and am told that I do it well. Our sessions would last approximately one hour. I enjoy licking not only pussy but ass as well. I am serious, clean, and safe and assure you discretion. I do not like to waste my time. Are you interested or not?"

I sat there for a moment stunned at his cut and dry speech, at the same time my clit was so hard and excited that it hurt. "I'm very interested," I finally said.

We went on to agree that we would meet at my place the following Wednesday afternoon. He didn't ask for a description, stating that age, race, and looks were unimportant, but I insisted on letting him know the basics; that I am a petite, long-haired blonde with an ample bottom and bosom. I figured that would help make the whole thing feel a little less impersonal.

Wednesday finally rolled around and I stood looking in the mirror, wondering what to wear for such an occasion.

I couldn't exactly call up a friend: "Hey Deb, what should I wear for my afternoon of pussy eating?"

I decided on something simple: a black V-neck top—he hadn't mentioned a cleavage fetish, but I figured it couldn't hurt—and a knee-length denim skirt with black boots. I didn't bother with panties—it seemed kinda pointless.

When he rang from downstairs, I did a quick primping of my long hair and touched up my lip gloss, making sure that my lips looked pink and wet—perfect for the occasion. My body trembled as I turned the doorknob. There he was, looking exactly as I had imagined, maybe a tad older. He was only a bit taller than I was and resembled my old science teacher. He was not someone that I would ever give a second glance to. He was old enough to be my father.

His hand was cold when he shook mine, barely cracking a smile. "Let's get started. Shall we stay here?" He pointed to the sofa in my living room.

"Sure," was all I could get out as he led me to the sofa and instructed me to sit down.

Almost clinically he told me he wanted to begin with my pussy. It felt so dirty: having this old, generic man in a respectable shirt and tie getting down on his knees in front of me using words like *pussy* and *cunt*. It was inappropriate and utterly exciting at the same time. I lifted my hips and ass off the sofa just enough for him to raise my skirt. I felt like a patient about to be examined by her doctor. I looked down and could see my clean-shaven cunt already glistening—had I ever been so juicy? He ran his hand over my damp, smooth skin, expressing his approval of my clean, bald mound. My knees shook as he pushed them farther apart and leaned in closer. I could feel his hot breath on my skin for a moment, and then he finally placed his open lips on mine. First some kisses all around my inner thighs and outer lips, then his fingers pulled at my delicate skin, parting my cunt lips until I could feel my pussy open wide—ready for his tongue.

I lay back with my eyes closed and just enjoyed the feeling of his tongue running up and down, all over my hot pussy. As he began sucking my clit, I sat up just enough to watch him. Every now and then he would glance up at me with his glasses steamed, his mouth and chin drenched with my juices. His expression was almost trancelike. I could see he was loving every lick.

Just as I would start to quiver, feeling myself ready to come, he would pause and change technique to put off my explosion for just a little longer. I could feel my hard nipples under my top as I watched him suck on my clit, squeezing my inner thighs with his fingers digging into my flesh, completely unaware of how rough he was being—but I was enjoying every second of it, more than anything I had ever experienced before.

I was mesmerized by the sight of this seemingly uptight man going at my cunt with such skill. I couldn't take it anymore and was about to explode when he took his face out from in between my legs and wiped the juice from his face.

"Have you ever had your asshole licked clean by a man's tongue?" he asked in that now familiar dry tone.

Before I got the chance to fully reply no, he instructed me to kneel down on the couch facing away from him. He raised my skirt again and used his hands to guide me into position, lifting my bare ass higher into the air. He spread my cheeks apart and quickly placed his mouth in between. His hot, wet tongue ran up and down my crack, his saliva running freely down toward my wet pussy. It felt amazing. I reached down with one hand and rubbed my clit as he slid his tongue into my asshole. It darted in and out quickly, and though I had never had anal sex before, I began to long for a hard cock to push into me. My whole body was on fire. I pushed my ass against his face, trying to get his tongue farther into me, at the same time fingering my cunt like mad. My insides began to tremble; I knew I was about to come, but it wasn't anything like the other times. It wasn't just my clit that was ready to explode; it was all of me.

He reached for the hand that was pumping in and out of my cunt and pushed it away, whispering into my ass, "Just let go…," and I did. My entire body trembled as I came, hard and fast. I could feel my buildup of juices flowing out of my cunt as my knees buckled and I collapsed downward, his tongue quickly moving to my cunt hole and lapping up everything that was coming out.

When the frenzy of my climax was over, I glanced lazily over at him and saw that his cock was out of his pants and he was wiping away his own come, some of which had gotten on his pants. I had been so sedated by my own pleasure I hadn't realized what eating my pussy was doing for him.

"That was amazing," I marveled, my cunt still throbbing from my climax. "Would you like me to do anything for you?" I asked, to show my sincere gratitude. "No, thank you. You gave me what I needed," was all he said.

I sat and watched him zip up his pants and get himself together; my legs were still open, my swollen cunt exposed. He stood up and thanked me, his face somber, and in that dry tone, he told me to give him a call the following week to arrange our next session. He disappeared through the door, leaving behind fifty dollars next to my telephone.

CRUISING

L. E. Yates

When I'm getting ready to go out on the
prowl I often get a feeling like the excitement
of being sick but without the nausea, like my
stomach lining is trying to peel away. It feels
good in the same way that inhaling sherbet
up your nose feels good, and believe me, I do
mean good. I pull on my heavy, steel-capped
biker boots, tucking them under my leather
trousers, and sling my battered black leather jacket over my white vest. One large silver spike rivets my ear. My hair is dark and
cropped short, snug against my head. I was
once told that I had eyes like flakes from an
iceberg—whatever that means. I'm wearing
bondage cuffs, tight confections of soft, supple, leather and stainless steel, around both
wrists for the constriction and sheer pleasure

of it. I know I'm looking good.

I bang the door behind me and stroll down the hill from my apartment. I live in an ancient cathedral city where small, beautiful medieval churches cluster and old flint-faced walls run into each other. Beautiful, but it's difficult to find the sex I need in this small, provincial place. I walk to the riverside, leaving little trails of iced breath in the dark air behind me. Dirty water slaps against the moorings and a line of grubby white cruising boats. I slouch my shoulders forward just a tiny bit and check that my jacket covers my small tits. It does. I step across the toll bridge and into the wooded park that marks the beginning of the local cruising area for gay men. I've become used to getting my kicks vicariously. I enjoy the ambiance. Strange men stalk between the trees, crunching leaves underfoot. Some of them walk dogs and feign nonchalance. I've even seen a few round here in business suits—no doubt, their wives are left waiting at home as they sully loafers in the mud and snag holes in pinstripe, rubbing against the rough bark of a tree as they're taken brutally and swiftly by a faceless man they met twenty seconds ago.

A whole new language of looks and come-ons develops. Rejection is as subtle as the tilt of a head. Tonight the air is spiced with the smoky tang of autumn and a sharp, slowly trickling sense of muted danger. Dark parkland, bushes, and trees lie ahead of me. Often I catch men fucking and stand and watch them—on their hands and knees, being shunted hard from behind, or half hidden by a bush having a thickening cock rammed into their warm mouths; even sitting on one of the forgotten park benches stroking each other's dicks.

Walking soundlessly, I reach the center of the park, continually checking the shadows and real obstacles that appear in my path. My clit is tingling. It aches from the recent sight of a youngish-looking man being fucked in the arse by a blond, heavy man in biker's leathers, whilst twisting his head around at the same time to service the throbbing, red-tipped erection of another kneeling man. I had to force myself to steal quietly away before they shot down his throat and arse, worried I'd forget myself and betray my presence by some involuntary noise of lust and jealousy mixed together. Now just ahead of me I see the outline of a tall, slim shape leaning against a tree. I prepare myself to walk past casually but my heart is bumping in my chest cavity. For the first time tonight I feel like I'm on display. The man is dressed in dark clothes, jeans and a jacket perhaps, and is leaning with one foot up against the tree. Something dangles from his right hand—oh, it's a dog leash. I relax slightly. I'm close enough to see that his hair is cut even shorter than mine. I look around but can't see the dog.

"Hey," the figure murmurs softly and I follow the sound without any real thought. I'm standing opposite now, face-to-face. For all my five feet seven I feel short. A kind of pleasurable sensation freezes my brain as the dog owner reaches forward with leather gloved hands and manipulates me so I'm facing the tree. I'm pushed so hard against it that I can feel the patterns of the bark pressing into my cunt. Hypnotized, I stay pressed against the thick trunk while the leash is used to fasten my hands together around the other side, securing me tightly to the tree.

"Cuffs—convenient," a concentrating voice mutters from the other side of the tree. The burning, stretching sensation in my arms as the final knot is tied restores some of my sense to me.

"What are you doing?" A pathetic and useless question.

The dog owner suddenly slams against me from behind, shoving me hard and nearly winding me.

"You should be quiet. I'm going to expose you…play with you…do what I like with you. If you want to be freed at the end don't make it necessary for me to use a gag or blindfold."

I stop squirming and trying to turn my head to see over my shoulder. That and my heavy breathing are taken for assent. All I can think is how I can now feel breasts against my back, and something harder, lower. The voice, although gruff, isn't quite low enough to be a man's, I realize. I can't believe it.

A cold, gloved hand reaches round and flips open the buttons of my trousers. Then my trousers are dragged down round my ankles. My assailant—whom I now know to be a woman—hoists my vest and jacket into a bundle around my shoulder blades. The chill air is like a slap to my whole body. My skin creeps up into gooseflesh. I'm naked, exposed, tied to a tree. I wonder how many people can see the luminous white of my flesh in the darkness, watching me just as I watched them. Leathermen, big daddies, bikers, circling around me with their cocks out, stroking themselves to hardness.

I can feel the zip of her jeans and hard metal of her belt buckle pressing into my bare arse and burning with the cold. Her hands reach round and grab the erect tips of my nipples as my legs are kicked apart—as wide as the trousers shackling my ankles will allow. She just spreads me wide and helps herself. My nipples are being plucked and pinched and teased into aching points of chafed skin. Then the pressure against my arse recedes and all my thoughts are concentrated in my nipples being worked so hard and grazed against the rough skin of the tree.

My cunt is dripping wet as I feel the cold tip of something long and very thick pressing tantalizingly against it. I try to open my legs wider but fail and I let out a visceral grunt of frustration. The freezing silicone head is rubbed up and down across the opening to my cunt, nudging up to my erect clit and slowly back down again to rest against the tight pucker of my arsehole.

"Maybe I should take you right here," she says, "like the little gay boy that you are, cruising around in the woods, looking for sex. Well, you've found it."

The head of her dick pushes against my clenched arsehole.

"No," I hear myself saying, "I've never been taken there." Can't she read the signs? I'm a top. I do not take it up the arse.

"Forbidding me, are you?" she croons. "We'll see."

Before I can reply she slams the thick dick she's packing into my cunt. Opening and stretching me, she gives my tight hole no time to adjust to the length and thickness. My cunt aches as she rams against the top of my cervix with her blunt, thick head, pulling nearly all the way out of me before thrusting back deep inside me. All I can feel is her in my cunt and her leather and metal bruising my buttocks. Anger at my enforced and unusual passivity and the sheer force of her cruel and energetic pounding begins to warm me.

I'm spread-eagled, wrapped around a tree and helpless. The muscles in my arms and stomach are being pulled to unbearable tautness as she works on me. I simply have to stand, spread and open, and let her impale my cunt repeatedly. I feel like I'm actually going to split down the middle but, despite myself, I can't help trying to push against her insistent, plunging dick.

"Oh, do you want some more?" She grabs me by the half-inch of hair on my head. "I'll give you what you want."

Slicked wet from my cunt she pulls her dick back and then pushes it into my virgin arse. It hurts like hell, more than sherbet up your nose. This is definitely a boundary. I feel like I'm going to dissolve, that I can't possibly bear her plunging in and out with long, hard strokes, or that I'll explode. But my sphincter tightens around every move she makes.

"That's right. Milk my good, big dick."

I'm just about to start screaming when her hand works its way round and insinuates itself against my clit. The cool leather strokes against my hard clit as she fills my arse again and again. I can't hold back and with my arse and clit being worked hard and my cunt empty and swollen to the night air I come so hard that all I can see is the rushing of red blood tissue before my eyes. It feels like she's come inside me, violating me further, flooding my walls, but I know this can't be true as it's only her silicone dick that is now being edged slowly out of me.

I sag against the tree as she plays the point of a knife up and down, up and down over my exposed flesh, before placing the handle in my hand. With difficulty I saw through the binding holding my wrists. Freed, I turn quickly round, rearranging my clothes. There is nothing but shadows and trees and bushes, a severed piece of leather and the rushing of the cold night air.

DEAL

Emerald

I don't dance the way I do on purpose. I'm
just moving the way my body is, well, moved
to. I don't really have any idea what I look
like, but it's been described by others as
seeming beyond control, as if the song has
taken over the essence of my existence for
its few minutes' duration. It's also been said
that some of those associated with me at those
particular moments suffer varying degrees of
embarrassment and judgment from what they
often see as these excessive spectacles.

Fair enough.

One thing I do know is that not everybody
chooses to dance the way I do. This is
something I honestly don't understand, because
I am overwhelmed when exposed to certain
songs, and I have trouble comprehending

why other people aren't similarly affected. All of this means that sometimes people notice me when I'm dancing. The bar where we were that night, for example, had a dance floor, but it wasn't really a dance bar—most of the time the floor stood empty. When one of my songs came on and I broke off a conversation with my friend Jacqueline in midsentence, she knew why. I would guess that helps explain what happened thereafter.

Breathing heavily and sweating, I returned to our table and gulped water. When I had caught my breath, I sat down, and Jacqueline and I resumed our conversation where it had left off. During a lull, I was glancing around at the crowd in the room when a guy about my age and definitely enough of a hottie to command my attention, approached me.

After a moment's hesitation, he said, "Hey, listen, you're an amazing dancer," his enthusiasm making him smile quickly.

"Oh, thanks." I nodded my acknowledgment.

"So listen," he continued and grinned somewhat impishly. "I happen to be throwing my best friend's bachelor party tomorrow night, and I was wondering if you'd be willing to strip for it."

I allowed myself a skeptical smile. Looking him up and down, I scooted my chair back a little.

"Haven't you already hired a stripper?" I asked.

"No, we decided we just weren't going to have one—too expensive. But when I saw you dance I just couldn't resist asking if we could hire you. I don't know if you dance professionally, but if you don't, you should. There are a couple of us here that'll be there, and we agreed we couldn't pass the opportunity up. I know you might think it's a pretty fucked-up idea and tell me to go to hell, but we thought it was worth a shot." The impish smile returned to his face. My expression hadn't changed.

I met his eyes. "How many guys are going to be there?"

He seemed a little flustered, and I knew he'd expected me to turn him down outright.

"About ten. Is that okay? About how much do you think this would run us? You'd definitely be worth it." He flashed his quick smile again.

I nodded and ignored both the question and the compliment. "How many of you are single—not counting the groom, of course?"

"Uh...let's see." He mentally counted and said, "Four. Four of us are single."

"That means no girlfriend, no attachment of any kind, right?"

"Yeah." He shrugged, somewhat confused.

"Okay." I leaned back in my chair and crossed my legs at the ankles. "Would you four be willing to fuck me when I'm done?"

His jaw dropped. It seemed to take him a few seconds to find his voice. "Excuse me?"

"Would the four single guys fuck me," I repeated.

"You mean—you mean at the same time? I mean—"

I laughed. "Yes, I mean at the same time. If you guys agree to gangbang me—by my rules"—I looked straight at him to make sure he understood the importance thereof—"that'd be payment enough for me, and I'll do it."

Though he had closed his mouth, his expression hadn't otherwise changed from the one of incredulity my counter-proposal had elicited.

"Well?"

"We can do that." He finally found his voice and regained his composure.

"Hm. I would think you might want to check with them first. But assuming they agree as well, I'm looking forward to it." I stood casually and shook his hand. "I'm Hailee."

"Devon." He appeared a bit dazed.

"Nice to meet you, Devon. I'll need the time and directions."

I didn't have to bring my own music; we agreed to three songs, which I picked and he said he had. The right music is not only important but imperative when I strip. It is, after all, what makes me dance. All I had to bring to Devon's place was myself and condoms, of which I made sure I had plenty. Devon and I had gone over the basic rules the night before when he gave me directions, and he seemed to understand them. I told him I'd go over them again before we got started.

I knocked on the door and waited. There was a fair amount of noise from behind the closed door, but it stopped when I stepped through the threshold.

Ten pairs of eyes beheld me, and I met each of them in turn.

"Hello," I said neutrally, stepping further in. Devon, who had answered the door, closed it, grinning, and shook my hand.

"Hey," he said. "Everybody, this is Hailee."

Some of the guys didn't seem to know what to do with themselves. The shy ones nodded, a couple of them not even meeting my eyes after the initial time. The more outgoing and even obnoxious ones were much more vocal. I narrowed my eyes slightly and looked at all of them, checking my intuition to make sure I wasn't getting any disrespectful vibes.

"So, you wanna get started?" Devon asked me.

"Sure." I shrugged, my intuition giving me a green light. "I'm ready when you are."

The noise level in the room had gradually returned. I noticed one of the louder guys say something to his buddy, and both of them burst out laughing. When they looked at me and noticed me staring at them, the laughter subsided slightly. I smiled coolly.

"We really appreciate you doing this for us," Devon said as he attended to the stereo.

"I hope to appreciate what four of you do for me later," I returned. The room once again fell silent. "Who are the lucky four, by the way?" I glanced around.

He pointed out the three others in the room. The loud one who'd made the comment to the guy beside him was one of them. That excited me, basically because he was hot. He had cropped blond hair that hung over his forehead and impudent blue eyes that winked at me when I met them. He appeared to be a few years younger than me, probably twenty-one or twenty-two. I took a deep breath, already getting turned on. The guy to whom he'd made the comment was also on the list. His brown eyes met mine. I smiled at him, and he seemed to forget whatever amusement loud blond boy beside him had shared minutes earlier. The fourth was one of the quieter men in the room. He smiled and glanced down when I smiled at him. As I continued to check out these four guys I'd be getting a taste of later, I determined this was definitely a satisfying arrangement for me so far.

"And this is Bob, the groom," Devon was saying, gesturing to the gorgeous man by his side. He smiled and stepped forward to shake my hand.

"Bob. It's nice to meet you. Hailee," I said, shaking his hand.

"You too," he said. "It's nice of you to do this for us."

Bob seemed like a genuinely nice guy, just like Devon. Apparently his future wife was a lucky woman. "No problem. And your bride doesn't mind, I take it? She does know, doesn't she?"

"Yeah, we told her about you. She says it's okay as long as you stay away from me. She trusts me though." Bob smiled; his manner was friendly and at ease.

I laughed. "Wonderful. That will be no problem. I'm happy to be here." I turned to the rest of the guys. "I'm ready when you are, boys. The sooner we get going, the sooner I get what *I* came for."

The opening notes of my first song started, and my expression changed. I turned away from all of them and walked to the back of the room. When the words started, I whirled around and started dancing. This didn't take a lot of effort from me; I danced the same way I would have danced had I been alone in the room. I yanked off the clip holding my hair up and tossed it to the corner of the room.

When I dance because I'm compelled to by the music, I'm not generally thinking consciously about what I'm doing. The music is literally moving me. This time, though, I tried to focus to some degree on what I was doing. Since the whole situation was really turning me on, I was touching myself a lot. I often run my hands over my body when I dance, but this time I was focusing a lot more on my breasts, running my hands over them and even squeezing them a time or two before running both hands through my hair or down over my hips. I looked every man in the room in the eye periodically;

some of them made eye contact, some didn't. I have to say, I was having a blast.

I'd worn an above-the-knee black skirt, lime green tank top, silver blouse (buttoned up), and matching red lace bra and thong. And of course I had on my knee-high, high-heeled black patent-leather boots. After a twirl, I kept my back to the group and danced back toward the back of the room, unbuttoning my shirt slowly as I did. My back still turned, I eased the blouse off my shoulders and down my body, listening to the yells and cheers as I did so. I allowed myself a small smile in the darkness of the room. Then I turned around, whipped the blouse all the way off, and threw it into the group. Hands went up all around.

I stopped paying attention to them and again lost myself in dancing. The second song started; I was slightly out of breath, and panted somewhat as Devon handed me a glass of water. I smiled my thanks, thinking mischievously that I would have perhaps preferred that he just pour it over me. Since he didn't, I took the liberty of doing it myself, tipping the glass toward me just above my breasts and pouring the contents down the front of my tank top. I let out a little cry and felt my nipples harden immediately as the icy liquid rushed down my warm skin.

I set the glass down and ran my hands up my soaked tank top as I moved to the music. Running them back down, I let one hand slip under my skirt and pull it up as I touched myself. The cheering sounded in my ears as I smiled and bit my lip. I ran my hands over my breasts and gripped the bottom of my tank top. Looking up, I met the eyes of my blond boy who'd made the comment to his buddy when I first got there. I stared hard at him, almost smiling, as I started to pull up my top. He stared back, his blue eyes just as hard. This turned me on, and

I bent deep at the knees and pulled my shirt over my head as I came back up. I threw it at him; he caught it without looking away from me. I raised my eyebrows slightly and whipped around, breaking eye contact.

Facing away from them again, I bent at the waist and placed my palms on the ground between my feet for a beat, then bent my knees and lowered myself to the floor. Rolling onto my back, I ran my hands slowly over myself and through my hair. Then I flipped over onto my stomach and got onto my hands and knees. I was getting wetter with each passing second anticipating what was to come after this show was over. Rising to my knees, I reached back and unzipped my skirt. I pulled it off me as I rose back to my feet. Now in only my red lace thong and bra with my black boots, I moved closer to my audience and in a quick motion jumped up onto the wooden coffee table.

The song I knew to be the last one started. It was a song that made me so hot I could hardly stand it. I ripped my hands through my hair and pulled my head back; I could feel the sweat on my chest mingling with the extra moisture from the ice water, now heated to the same temperature as my skin. Letting go of my hair, I reached for the back of my bra and unhooked it. The shy guy of my four, a boyishly attractive one with curly brown hair, was actually looking at me when I met his eyes. He looked away quickly. I smiled.

I turned around and pulled my bra off. Jumping off the coffee table, I threw the bra over my shoulder and crossed my arms over my breasts. Then I turned back toward them, my long hair falling across my face and over my arms. I looked at every last man in the room before suddenly pulling my arms away and running my hands down my body. My breasts bounced around as I whirled and sashayed, and I grabbed and squeezed them, running my fingers softly over my hard nipples as I thought about who else would be touching them soon.

Finally I reached for my thong. I touched the sides of it, pulling it away from me and teasing for a moment as I pretended to pull it down and then pulled it back up. Expressions of protest made me smile. Slowly I hooked a finger through each side of it and eased it down my legs and over my boots. Not one of them was looking at my eyes now.

I kicked the thong to the side and finished dancing to the song. When it ended, I stood in front of them, out of breath and hands on my hips, while they cheered for me. I reached for my silver blouse and pulled it around myself. A few protests emerged as I did so.

I laughed. "Use your memory, boys."

Devon came over to me. Before he could say anything, I pressed up against him and said in his ear, "It's time for my part of the deal."

He nuzzled my ear and put his arms around me. "I'll show you to the bedroom and then get the other three."

I waited in the bedroom, lying on my side on the bed. I kept my blouse around me. By now I felt in control of this entire situation, but I was certainly still going to go over the rules before things got started.

Someone knocked, and I chuckled and said, "Come in."

Devon entered, followed by the three other single men at the party. I smiled at the brown-haired, shy one. He seemed slightly uncomfortable.

"Are you sure you all want to do this?" I asked seriously. I wasn't into having anyone do anything he (or she) didn't want to. All of them nodded, including the shy one, so I smiled.

"Wonderful." I looked at the loud blond one, who did not hesitate to look back. His blue eyes held unchecked lust and desire. I shivered. "Now tell me your names again."

"Oh," Devon said. "This is Chad," he indicated the blond one, who was still looking at me, "this is Brent," the brown-eyed shy one, "and this is Greg." Greg had dark brown hair, worn spiked with a lot of gel. He was the one Chad had joked with when I first came in. I smiled again.

"Okay guys, here are the rules." I got up and stood by the bed, making sure I had their attention. "First of all, no one gets in me without a condom." I indicated the box on the nightstand and received nods all around. "Secondly, it goes without saying that I am in control of what happens to me. If at any point things get out of hand and something happens that I don't want to have happen and I tell you to stop and you don't—I will not hesitate to kill someone." I didn't smile. This is entirely true, and I can't think of a better way to show them how serious I am than being honest.

I got three surprised looks—I'd already shared this rule with Devon—but I continued. "That's not meant to be alarming, it's just the truth. I have no problem taking someone's life who is trying to force me to do something I don't want to do. Nothing happens that I don't want to happen. Got it?"

Devon looked at the other three, and everyone assented. I felt relatively comfortable that there would be no problems.

"Great. That said..." I paused. I didn't want them to be inhibited either. I certainly wanted this to be fun. It was just important that I remained in control. My voice lowered. "That said, I like it a little rough." I looked at Chad, whose eyes narrowed slightly. I was getting wet again already. "I like to have my ass smacked and my hair pulled and my tits grabbed, and I *love* to have hot come shot all over my body." Chad reached down and ran a strong hand over the noticeable erection beneath his jeans, still looking at me. My breathing got deeper. It was about time to start.

"Okay," I said breathlessly. "Let's go." I grabbed Devon and kissed him hard. He wrapped his arms around me immediately and pulled the blouse off me. I felt the other three crowd around beside and behind me, and numerous hands started touching me. I gasped as Devon moved down and started sucking my nipples.

Chad, who I deduced was behind me, reached around my right hip and slipped his hand between my legs. He slid a finger in my slick pussy, and I cried out and clutched Devon's shoulders. Pulling away from them all, I lay down on the bed and spread my legs, running my hands down the inside of my thighs.

"Somebody get a condom on and fuck me," I ordered.

Devon nodded at Greg. After ripping one open and sliding it down his hard cock, Greg climbed on the bed and got between my legs. Looking at my wet pussy, he gripped my knees and pulled them further apart. I arched my back and bit my lip. "Fuck me, baby," I whispered.

Greg pushed his huge cock into me, and I howled. Devon had stepped back to watch, so I grabbed Brent's hand, as he was standing closest to me, and pulled him toward me. "Give me your big cock to suck on," I commanded. Obliging, he moved to the edge of the bed where my head was turned toward him, and his cock found my lips. I opened my mouth wide and heard him groan as I took his hard length in my mouth. Moaning as much as I could with Brent's cock filling my mouth, I felt Greg pumping me hard and someone else grab my tits from my other side. I pulled away from Brent's cock for a moment, stroking it with my hand while I turned to see who was on my other side. Devon hovered above me, massaging my tits with one hand and stroking himself with the other. I looked for Chad. He stood near Brent, still watching.

Reaching up, I pulled Greg down and flipped us over and straddled him. I rode him hard as I turned to Devon and told him to fuck my ass. He moved in and got behind me on the bed. I gasped as I felt him ease his thick cock into my ass. The combination of Devon working my ass while Greg pounded my hot pussy quickly had me in a frenzy. Brent was still beside me, and I turned my head and took his cock in my mouth again. After several minutes, with Devon grabbing my tits from behind, I knew I was going to come any second, but Devon beat me to it. He pulled out of my ass and yanked his condom off, and I could hear him moaning as he came on the small of my back.

That did it for me. I pulled my mouth off Brent's cock and screamed as I came for the first time that night. Devon slapped my ass as I did, which made me scream even more. I saw Chad tap Greg's shoulder, and Greg flipped us over and thrust into me for a few seconds before pulling out and grabbing my hips to turn me over. I got on my hands and knees, and Greg started fucking me from behind while Chad knelt in front of me so I could suck his big cock. Greg reached around and massaged my clit while he pounded me. When I felt him grab and pull my hair, I pulled away from Chad and came again, ripping my long nails down the sheets and burying my face in a pillow.

I noticed Brent now kneeling on the bed beside me; I reached over and stroked his rock-hard cock and looked up into his eyes. He reached down and fondled my tits. Soon I felt Greg pull out of me, and he grabbed my shoulder and pulled me around hard so he could come on my tits. Now on my back, I moaned and smeared the hot come all over my tits and up my neck. Brent straddled my face and pushed his cock between my lips, somewhat surprising me, but I was more than happy to oblige him as he pumped my mouth.

I felt Chad between my legs then, and he lifted my ankles high in the air as he pushed his big cock into me. I kept my eyes fastened on Brent's until he suddenly withdrew from my mouth and came on my face. Hot come drizzled over my neck as I threw my head back and listened to him moan. Breathing heavily, he ran a hand through my hair and smiled at me, then hoisted himself off the bed.

Now it was just Chad and me. He looked hard into my eyes as he pumped me furiously, and I grabbed my ankles and held them out to each side as I looked back. Just watching Chad while he fucked me almost made me come. With each of his hard thrusts, I grunted louder, and he reached down and circled my clit with his thumb. It took only a few seconds of that to make me come again. Arching my back and screaming, I grabbed frantically at the sheets above my head for a few seconds before I let go of them and grabbed my bouncing tits.

"Yes, fuck me, Chad," I gasped as I reached for his hands. He laced his fingers through mine and slammed my hands down on either side of my head, pounding my wet pussy even harder. I closed my eyes as I howled and writhed beneath him. A few minutes later, I felt him pull out and opened my eyes as he pulled the condom off and came all over my stomach. I reached down and smeared it up to my tits, still feeling the aftershocks of orgasm.

He finally let go of his dripping cock and met my eyes, smiling at me for the first time. I laughed breathlessly as he winked and lifted himself off of me and off the bed. The other three guys sat in chairs around the room, recovering. I bit my lip and turned over onto my stomach, facing them, and smiled. Devon handed me a couple towels and smiled back.

I opened the bedroom door to see six guys suspiciously close to it scramble into various casual positions.

"Oh hello, Hailee." Bob smiled at me. "We almost forgot you were here."

Laughing, I congratulated Bob again and headed across the room. "Thanks again, guys," I called over my shoulder. When I reached the door, I opened it and turned back in. "And boys. Do let me know the next time you all get together like this." With a wink, I pulled the door shut behind me.

There is nothing like successfully living out your favorite fantasy.

FOUR ON THE FLOOR

Alison Tyler

We weren't very nice about it. That was the surprising part. I expected the cliché of scented oils and the gilded candlelight ambiance and the slippery limbs entwined. But how we acted afterward was unforeseen. Alone together, reliving the night, Sam and I were truly cruel. And here I was, operating under a false impression for so many years.

You see, I always thought I was a nice girl.

Others reliving the experience might choose to focus on the way Sheila's gray-blue eyes had lit up when I'd pressed my mouth to her freshly shaved pussy, or the look on her husband Richard's craggy but handsome face as he started to slowly stroke his long, uncut cock. But not this girl. The best part of the evening for me was the laughter with Sam afterward, giggling all the way home about the freaks we'd spent the evening with. The freaks we'd just fucked.

They were decades older than us, and richer by far, and they'd run a charming ad at the back of the *Guardian*. Filled with dizzy anticipation, we met for drinks, to check out the chemistry factor. Sizing up potential fuck partners is a heady business. Nobody else in the trendy after-work bar crowd knew that we were responding to a personal. Not the cute curly-haired bartender. Not the female executives lined up against the wall like pretty maids all in a row. The thought of what we were actually there for made me giddy with excitement, and desire showed rather brightly in my dark eyes.

The woman said I was pretty. Her husband agreed with an anxious nod. All evening long, they looked at me rather than Sam, and I knew why. Sam is tough. He has short, razor-cut hair and a gingery goatee. If you were to meet him in a back alley, you'd offer him your wallet in a heartbeat. You'd beg him to take it, the way I beg him to take things from me every night.

The couple didn't understand Sam. So they talked to me instead.

"So pretty," the woman repeated. "Like Snow White."

I grinned and drank my cosmo, then licked my cherry-glossed lips in the sexiest manner I could manage, leaving the tip of my tongue in the corner of my mouth for one second too long. Iridescent sparkles lit up my long dark hair. Multicolored body glitter decorated my pale skin. I wore serpentine black leather pants and a white baby-T with the word *SINNER* screaming across the chest in deep scarlet. There was an unspoken emphasis on how young I was in comparison to the woman. She was holding firm in her midforties, while

I was just barely getting used to being in my early twenties. Her entire attitude was both calculating and clearly at ease, obvious in the way she held court in our booth, in the way she ordered from the waiter without even looking up.

"Two Kettle-One martinis, another cosmo, another Pilsner."

I was her opposite, bouncy and ready, a playful puppy tugging on a leash. More than that, I was bold from sensing how much they wanted us, and I was wet from how much I wanted Sam. When he put one firm hand on my thigh under the table, I nearly swooned against him. We'd be ripping the clothes off each other in hours.

After drinking away the evening, we made a real date with the rich couple for the following weekend, a date at their place, where they promised to show us their sunken hot tub, wraparound deck, and panoramic view of the city. In cultured voices, they bragged to us about the gold records from his music-producing days, and her collection of antique Viennese perfume bottles accumulated with the assistance of eBay. But although I listened politely, I didn't care about their money or what it could buy. All I wanted was all Sam wanted, which was simple: four on the floor.

We had done the act already, nearly a year before, with a lower-class duo Sam found for us on the Internet. The woman was thirty-eight, the man twenty-six. They'd been together for two years, and had wanted to sample another couple as a way of enhancing their already wild sex life. After dinner at a local pizzeria, and two bottles of cheap red wine, Pamela and I retreated to the ladies' room to show each other our tattoos. Hers was a dazzling fuchsia strawberry poised right below her bikini line. When she lifted her white dress, I saw that not only was she pantyless, but she'd been very recently spanked. She blushed becomingly as I admired her glowing red rear cheeks, where lines from Andy's belt still shone in stark relief against her coppery skin.

"He gave me what-for in the parking lot," she confessed. "Told me that he wanted me to behave during dinner."

"What would he think of this?" I asked, stroking her still-warm ass with the open palm of my hand.

"I think he'd approve," she grinned.

I gave her a light slap on her tender skin, and she turned around and caught me in a quick embrace, lifting my dress slowly so that she could see my own ink.

Teasingly, I turned to show her the cherries on my lower back, then pulled down my bikinis to reveal the blue rose riding on my hip. She traced my designs with the tips of her fingers, and I felt as if I were falling. Her touch was so light, so gentle, and in moments we started French-kissing, right there in the women's room at Formico's, while I could only imagine what the men were doing. Speaking of macho topics to one another, sports and the recent war, while growing harder and harder as they waited for us to return to the red-and-white-checked table.

Sam and I followed the duo to their Redwood City apartment, and into their tiny living room, overshadowed by a huge-screen TV and a brown faux-leather sofa. Pamela had her tongue in my asshole before my navy blue sleeveless dress was all the way off, and my mouth was on Andy's mammoth cock before he could kick off his battered black motorcycle boots.

The TV stayed on the whole time we were there. Muted, but on. We had crazy sex right on the caramel-colored shag rug in front of it, while heavy metal bands played for us in silence. It was like doing it on stage with Guns N' Roses. Surreal, but not a turn-off.

I remember a lot of wetness—her mouth, his mouth, her pussy. I remember Sam leaning against the wood-paneled wall at one point in the evening and watching, just watching the three of us entwined, the TV-glow flickering over us, my slim body stretched out between our new lovers. I felt beloved as their fingers stroked me, as they took turns tasting me, splitting my legs as wide as possible and getting in between. I held my arms over my head and Sam bent down and gripped my wrists tight while Pamela licked at me like a pussycat at a saucer of milk.

Scenes flowed through the night, lubricated by our red-wine daze, and we moved easily from one position to another. Pamela bent on her knees at Sam's feet and brought her mouth to his cock. I worked Andy, bobbing up and down, and after he came for the first time, I moved over to Pamela's side, so we could take turns drinking from Sam. I was reeling with the wonder of it. The illusion that anything was possible. Any position, any desire.

"You like that?" Andy asked when I returned to his side, pointing to Pamela as she sucked off my husband. "You like watching?"

I nodded.

"What else do you like?"

"I like that you spanked her," I confessed in a soft voice.

"Ah," he smiled. "So you're a bad girl, too."

My blush told him all he needed to know, and soon I was upended over his sturdy lap, and the erotic clapping sounds of a bare-ass spanking rang through the room. Andy punished me to perfection, not letting up when I started to cry and squirm, making me earn the pleasure that flooded through me. Sam filled Pamela's mouth while watching another man tan my hide.

Andy was a true sadist, which I could appreciate. He had a pair of shiny orange-handled pliers which he used like a magician on his girlfriend's teacup tits. She didn't cry or scream; she moaned. He twisted the pliers harder, and her green eyes became a vibrant emerald, as if she'd found some deep hidden secret within herself, and as if that secret gave her power. Andy told us stories of how he liked to spank her with his hand or a belt or paddle. Sometimes he used a wooden ruler. Sometimes he used whatever was nearby. He told us detailed stories of how he fucked her up the ass; how he made her bend over and part her cheeks for him, holding herself open as wide as possible and begging him for it. He liked to lube her up good, and then pour a handful of K-Y into his fist and pump his cock once or twice before taking her. The size of his cock in her back door would often make her cry, but it was a good sort of cry, he explained. Pain and pleasure were entwined in everything they did. Andy's stories made me more excited, and we kept up our games all night long.

Sam and I had fun with that couple, and we didn't laugh afterward. We fucked. Not like bunnies, which are cute and soft and sweet. We fucked like us. Hard and raw and all the time. Sam's large hand slapped down on my ass, connecting over and over as he relived the night. "You little cock slut," he said, his voice gravelly and low. "Your mouth was all hungry for him. You couldn't get enough." I would be red and sore after our sessions, and I relished every mark, every pale plum-colored bruise, every memory. The night was fuel for a year's worth of fantasies. We got precisely what we wanted, even though we never saw them again, because the woman turned out to be mildly insane. She called and called after our one-night stand. She emailed that she was in love with me, that she was desperate to see me. But Sam and I didn't want love. We wanted something much less involved but much more momentarily intense: four on the floor.

With Sheila and Richard, we got a great deal more than we bargained for. A gourmet dinner—delivered by a local party service—that dragged on for hours. A tour of their two-story house and their walk-in closets. Close-up views of their his-and-hers Armanis. We received an in-depth explanation of how their pure pedigreed dogs, who were busy in the corner of the living room chewing on pigs' ears, had been "de-barked." Their voice boxes had been removed, which had caused the dogs so much trauma, the pets were now on puppy Prozac.

These appearance-obsessed people were the ones we were about to have sex with. I had a difficult time picturing it. Yes, she was attractive, although *cool* was a better word. Yes, I liked how distinguished he looked in his open-necked crisp white shirt and pressed khakis with the ironed crease down the center. He was so different from Sam with his faded Levi's and dangling silver wallet chain. But they were trying to win us over, and somehow that made me feel hard and bristly inside. Didn't stop us from getting busy, though—choosing a spot far away from those demented dogs and peeling our clothes off. Richard didn't fuck me. He sat nearby and stroked my sleek dark hair out of my eyes and said he wanted to watch. Sheila had on a black velvet catsuit, and she stripped it off with one practiced move and was naked, her platinum hair rippling over her shoulders, her body gleaming chestnut in the candlelight. She stood for a moment, holding the pose, waiting for applause or flashbulbs.

Sam took his cue from Richard at first, backing away, watching while Sheila courted me. Sheila had obviously done this before. She strode to my side and helped to undress me. She cooed softly, admiringly, as she undid my bra and pulled it free, as she slid my satin dove-gray panties down my thighs. Her fingers inspected me all over, as if she was checking to see that a purchase she'd made was acceptable. She kissed wetly into the hollow of my neck and caressed my breasts with her long, delicate fingers, tweaking my rosy nipples just so to make them erect. Then she spread me out on the luxurious multicolored living room rug and started to kiss along the basin of my belly. I had one second to wonder why it is that ménages never take place in beds before I sighed, arched my back, parted my legs for her, and closed my eyes. She turned her body, lowered herself on me, and let me taste her.

Everything about her body felt cool, like polished foil. Her skin. Her lips. Her tangy juices when they flooded out to meet my tongue. We sixty-nined for the men, and for a moment, I was won over. I was fine, alert, and happy. With my mouth on the older woman's pussy, and my hands stroking her perfect silky body, I lost myself in momentary bliss. She was exotically perfumed, a scent I didn't recognize but knew must have been imported from Europe. She even tasted expensive. But sex levels out any playing field. I might only have been able to afford CoverGirl dime-store cosmetics rather than Neiman Marcus special blends, but I could find her swollen clit easily, and that's all that mattered. I teased it out from between her perfectly shaved pussy lips. I sucked hard, and then used my tongue to trace ring around the rosy.

When I felt Sam's eyes on me, I turned my head to look at him. He gave me a wink, as if to let me know that he approved, and then he nodded forward with his head for me to continue. I could already hear his voice in my mind: "You liked your mouth all glossy with pussy juices, didn't you, girl? You liked the way she tasted, all slippery and wet?"

But then Sheila started to direct, positioning my body on all fours, before grabbing a carved wooden box from under the coffee table and pulling out a variety of sex toys. This wasn't like Andy lifting his pliers off the oval-shaped coffee table, an unexpected turn-on. This was planned; I could tell. We had been carefully chosen to star in a prewritten fantasy of Sheila's. A fantasy in which she was the star and I was her assistant, her underling, her protégé. And even as she buckled on the thick, pink strap-on, I felt myself withdraw.

Still, we fucked.

She took me from behind, holding tightly to my long black hair, and rode me. Her well-manicured fingertips gripped firmly near the base of my scalp, holding me in place. Sam stared into my eyes as I was pounded by this icy woman, and then he came close, his cock out, and placed the head on my full bottom lip. I heard Sheila hiss something—Sam was taking charge and she didn't like it. But she also didn't know Sam. Sam would have none of her noise, the way she would have none from her dogs. He fucked my mouth fiercely while she fucked my cunt, and Richard, silent and somewhere off inside himself, tugged on his dick and watched us all.

Sheila had oils that she spread on me with the finesse of a masseuse, and soon we were drippy and glistening in the golden light. She had sturdy metal nipple clamps and assorted colorful dildos, vibrating devices, and butt plugs. She arrayed her collection and went to work. And Sam let it all happen. This was far different, and far less spontaneous, than our experience with Pamela and Andy, but we'd use it. We'd go with it. There were four of us, after all, and we were there.

I came when she oiled me up between my rear cheeks and slowly slipped in a petal-pink butt plug, her knowing fingers working between my thighs to tickle my clit as she filled my ass with the toy. I came again when Sam jacked himself hard and let loose in my mouth, filling me up with his cream as Sheila fucked me from behind. I jammed my fingers between my legs, working my own clit to come a final time when Richard, so distant, lowered his head and shuddered, his body wracked with tremors as he climaxed a white fountain up onto his hard belly.

But in the car on the way home at two A.M., still reeking of imported essential oils, still throbbing from the poundings I'd taken, I started to giggle. And then Sam started to laugh out loud.

"Voice boxes removed," he said, shaking his head as he drove along the empty highway.

"Crazy."

"So much Armani," he snorted.

"And gold records."

"And cigars."

"And their view."

"And their money."

And we didn't see them again, even though they called for weeks afterward. Even though they fell a little bit in love with us, as had Pamela and Andy. Because Sam and I weren't looking for love. We had plenty of that. We were looking for one thing only. And somehow I was sure that we'd find it again once I placed a personal ad of our own:

Happily married twosome seeks similar couple for debauchery. For intensity. For four on the floor.

ABOUT THE AUTHORS

SYDNEY BEIER recently returned to Seattle after a two-and-a-half-year stint living in Germany with her husband. They now contemplate existence *auf* English from a little hill just northwest of the Space Needle. In addition to writing, Sydney dabbles in photography. Her images have been featured in Alaskan tourism publications and newspapers. Her fiction has been published at Erotica Readers and Writers Association, *Clean Sheets,* and in Logical Lust's ebook, *Eternally Erotic.*

Originally from New Zealand, MAGENTA BROWN is based in London where she writes for newspapers and magazines, and for film and television—usually under her real name. Having also trained and worked as an actress, it's to be expected that Magenta has also done time as a phone and text sex operator.

RACHEL KRAMER BUSSEL (www.rachelkramerbussel.com) is senior editor at *Penthouse Variations* and a contributing editor at *Penthouse,* where she writes the "Girl Talk" column. She is the editor of *Up All Night: Adventures in Lesbian Sex* and *Naughty Spanking Stories from A to Z, Volumes 1* and *2;* she writes the "Lusty Lady" column for the *Village Voice;* and she is an interviewer at Gothamist.com. Her writing has been published in over sixty erotic anthologies, including *Best American Erotica 2004* and *2006,* as well as *AVN, Bust,* Cleansheets.com, *Curve, Diva, Girlfriends,* Mediabistro.com, the *New York Post, On Our Backs,* Oxygen.com, *Punk Planet, Rockrgrl,* the *San Francisco Chronicle, Time Out New York,* and *Velvetpark.*

ELIZABETH COLDWELL has been writing and editing erotica for longer than she actually cares to remember. Her work has appeared in anthologies including *Best S/M Erotica; Leather, Lace and Lust;* and *Sex at the Sports Club.*

BONNIE DEE is a young fortysomething wife, mother, and secretary, who has discovered her inner writer over the past couple of years. As her fiction pieces grew racier, she discovered that her smutty stuff had a name—erotica. She's had a piece accepted at *Penthouse Variations* and a story, "Sports Widow," will appear in the upcoming anthology *Sex at the Sports Club.* Erotic writing is a great release and now that she's "come out" to her immediate family, she's even more comfortable with making it a part-time career.

EMERALD has been a writer since age seven, though her repertoire did not begin to include erotica until her early twenties. Originally from Iowa, she has studied creative writing at Eastern Washington University in Spokane and holds a master's degree in political management from George Washington University in Washington, DC. She spends much of her time writing fiction (both erotic and not) and poetry, as well as working as an activist for reproductive rights and other socially progressive issues. Currently she resides with her cat in Rockville, Maryland, and makes her living in the nonprofit arena in Washington, DC.

Decadent, devilish, and *delightful* are three words that have been used to describe the work of K. L. GILLESPIE. She wrote her first story, at age seven, about a child-eating nun, and since then she has worked as a music journalist, art gallery curator, and screenwriter. Her work has appeared in several magazines, from *TANK* to *Moist,* and in Mitzi Szereto's anthology *Wicked.* At the moment she is working night and day on her eagerly anticipated first novel, *Jesus Loves Penge.*

EVA HORE has been widely published on the Web and in many magazines, such as *Hustler, Forum,* and *New Cummers,* and in the anthologies *The Mammoth Book of Erotic Fantasies, Skin Deep 2, Delicate Friction, Best Lesbian Fiction 2005, My Wife and Her Lovers, Erotica 5,* and *Bettina Can't Help It.* Her first novel, *Sexual Deception,* and two novellas are all due for release in 2005.

GENEVA KING is an active member of the Erotica Readers and Writers Association, and her work has been published in *Erotic Fantasy: Tales of the Paranormal.* She intends to publish a collection of her stories, if her professors ever give her enough time to do so. You can visit her website at www.angelfire.com/empire2/gking/index.html.

TERESA LAMAI lives in the Pacific Northwest. When she stopped dancing, she started writing fiction, and it swiftly became a full-blown obsession. Her writing can be found in *Best Lesbian Erotica,* and at CleanSheets.com and the website of the Erotica Readers and Writers Association. She is currently working on her first novel.

JEAN ROBERTA lives on the Canadian prairie, where she teaches mandatory first-year English classes at the local university and writes erotic stories, articles, reviews, and rants. Her monthly column, "In My Jeans," can be found on the website Bluefood.com. Her stories have appeared in previous editions of *Best Women's Erotica* (2000, 2003, 2005) and *Best Lesbian Erotica* (2000, 2001, 2004, 2005), as well as *Best of Best Lesbian Erotica 2, Hot Lesbian Erotica,* and *The Merry XXXmas Book of Erotica.*

After a long career as a teacher and as writer of a successful series of children's books, CATE ROBERTSON recently turned her attention to erotica. Her fiction has been published online at CleanSheets.com and ScarlettLetters.com, as well as in print anthologies. Cate lives in Canada with her husband.

With a bit of talent, a fairly filthy mind, and a day job that brings her into contact with a vast array of potential characters, ADRIE SANTOS has been slowly turning her dream into her work, with several stories in print in Canada, the United States, and abroad. Though the erotica anthology market seems to have welcomed her with open arms (and legs!), Adrie is currently working on a book, and dabbling in other genres with hopes of being able to live her dream full-time in the near future.

LEE SKINNER's alter ego is a mommy-track attorney who writes legal articles and police college textbooks. "He" idly wonders why "his" best erotica is always written in a first-person male voice, but as a freelancer, "he" can't afford the psychotherapy needed to find out.

DONNA GEORGE STOREY finds writing to be the best therapy there is. Her fiction has appeared in *The Gettysburg Review*; AGNI.com; *Clean Sheets*; *Scarlet Letters*; *Taboo: Forbidden Fantasies for Couples*; *Foreign Affairs: Erotic Travel Tales*; *The Mammoth Book of Best New Erotica 4*; *Best Women's Erotica 2005*; and *Best American Erotica 2006*. A story published in *Prairie Schooner* received special mention in *Pushcart Prize Stories 2004*. Visit her at www.DonnaGeorge-Storey.com.

ALISON TYLER has written more than fifteen explicit novels, including *Learning to Love It, Strictly Confidential, Sweet Thing, Sticky Fingers, Something About Workmen,* and *Rumors.* Her stories have appeared in anthologies including *Sweet Life* and *Sweet Life 2; Taboo; Best Women's Erotica 2002, 2003,* and *2005; Best of Best Women's Erotica; Best Fetish Erotica; Best Lesbian Erotica 1996; Wicked Words 4, 5, 6, 8,* and *10; Sex at the Office;* and *Sex on Holiday,* as well as in *Playgirl* magazine. She is the editor of *Batteries Not Included, Heat Wave, Best Bondage Erotica, Best Bondage Erotica 2, Three-Way, Naughty Fairy Tales from A to Z,* the *Naughty Stories from A to Z* series, the *Down & Dirty* series, *Naked Erotica,* and *Juicy Erotica.*

ALICIA WAG's work has been published in newspapers, magazines, and literary journals across the country. She writes articles, nonfiction, and fiction, but enjoys creating erotica most of all. She lives in Massachusetts with her husband and children.

SASKIA WALKER (www.saskiawalker.co.uk) is a British author who has had short erotic fiction published on both sides of the pond. You can find her work in *Seductions: Tales of Erotic Persuasion; Sugar and Spice; More Wicked Words; Wicked Words 5* and *8; Sextopia; Naughty Stories from A to Z, Volumes 3* and *4; Naked Erotica; Taboo: Forbidden Fantasies For Couples; Three-Way; Best Bondage Erotica 2; The Merry XXXmas Book of Erotica; Stolen Moments: Erotic Interludes;* and *Stirring Up a Storm.* She also writes erotic romance, and her first novel, *Along for the Ride,* and a novella, *Summer Lightning,* will be published in 2005.

JORDANA WINTERS's writing has appeared online at thermo-erotic.com, eXtasybooks.com, and free-sex-story.org. When not hiding behind her computer telling naughty tales, Jordana is a somewhat quiet and reserved white-collar worker. Her interests are reading, writing, and pissing people off. Currently she is working on completing her first novel, *Bound*, a BDSM love story. Visit her at http://jordanawinters.tripod.com.

L. E. YATES is a twenty-three-year-old student, currently working on the side as a freelance journalist and writer in East Anglia in the United Kingdom. "Cruising" is her first foray into the dirty and demanding twilight world, or so she likes to imagine it, of women's erotica. Yates is interested in the imaginative loophole sex creates out of the boring contract of everyday life. In her spare time she enjoys visiting urban woodlands and pretending to walk her dog.

ABOUT THE EDITOR

VIOLET BLUE is a professional sex educator, sex columnist, female porn expert, pro-porn pundit, and the Assistant Editor at Fleshbot.com. She is the editor of *Sweet Life: Erotic Fantasies for Couples, Sweet Life 2, Taboo: Forbidden Fantasies for Couples,* and *Best Sex Writing 2005,* and the author of *The Ultimate Guide to Fellatio, The Ultimate Guide to Cunnilingus, The Ultimate Guide to Adult Videos,* and *The Ultimate Guide to Sexual Fantasy.* Blue has appeared on Playboy TV's *Sexcetera,* NPR, and CNN, and she has been featured in such publications as *Esquire; Cosmopolitan; O, The Oprah Magazine; Salon.com; Newsweek;* and *Wired.* Visit her at www.tinynibbles.com.